LONE WOLF

SHELLEY MUNRO

Lone Wolf

Print ISBN: 978-1-99-106318-2
Digital ISBN: 978-0-9951026-2-0

Cover: Kim Killion, The Killion Group, Inc.

Munro Press, New Zealand.

First Munro Press electronic publication August 2017

First Munro Press print publication March 2023

For Paul.

INTRODUCTION

R.J. BLAKE TRAINS YOUNG werewolves in the old ways—giving them a taste of how it was before the introduction of the shift-suppressing drugs that allow their kind to live secretly among humans. He expects nothing out of the ordinary with his new batch of students. Until sexy, smart, aggravating-as-hell Corey Wilson arrives. Older than the others, son of a powerful Los Angeles pack leader, Corey is an instant temptation he cannot afford.

The last thing Corey wants is three months stuck in the Yellowstone wilderness, followed by the stifling life his father has mapped out for him. One glimpse of R.J.

though, sparks a determination to seduce the older man before he leaves. Yet as R.J. guides him through the sometimes terrifying process of rediscovering his heritage, a deepening respect calls to his artistic soul and fuels a burst of creativity.

When their time comes to an end, Corey senses hesitation behind R.J.'s insistence that theirs was simply a summer fling. Inspiring him to take a leap of faith with consequences neither of them saw coming. A dangerous plot that reaches from the heart of their love to the highest office in the land...

Warning: This book contains a young werewolf intent on seduction, an older werewolf determined to resist said seduction, werewolf politics and brutality, a little spilled blood, and hot, naked manlove in the great outdoors.

CHAPTER ONE

"R.J., KEEP AN EYE on Corey Wilson while he's here at Yellowstone. He's older than the rest of the kids and I don't want him leading them astray. You've read his file?"

"Yes, sir." Hiding a grin from his boss, R.J. snapped a salute and turned his attention back to the arrivals section of the airport. He'd read Corey's file, along with those of the other teens in this intake for the Yellowstone National Park program.

A loud snort emerged from Hal. "Smart-ass. I don't want anything to go wrong with this kid. His father runs the L.A. pack."

"You worry too much. The kid isn't any different from the others. He's here to learn and enjoy himself. They want to experience the forbidden and shift to wolf. Break a few rules."

Officially, he and Hal were here to pick up the recruits for the summer season at the park. In reality, they intended to collect the latest group of city werewolves who paid big bucks to gain experience in the wild, their park holding the sole license to provide an exclusive few with exposure to their wolves. R.J. bounced with anticipation and the glint in Hal's eyes suggested the same enthusiasm filled him. The raw and gritty knowledge of their werewolf heritage never failed to change the kids, usually for the better.

"I forgot to tell you. We managed one scholarship kid this intake," Hal said. "A late addition. I'll give you his file once we return to camp."

"Good." R.J. concentrated on the arrivals area, a sense of pride filling him. His small contribution to the scholarship was a way of showing his thanks to Hal. Not every kid managed to grow up with a mentor like him. Most wolves didn't lead the same unfettered life as him either or comprehend the savage joy of running free. A hundred years ago, maybe, but times changed.

Current werewolf law forbade unregulated shifting.

Passengers started to exit, and they sprang to attention. R.J. displayed his sign while Hal readied his clipboard, although it was easy to spot the city kids among the other passengers. For once, the entire group was arriving on the same plane, the kids flying in from Los Angeles to spend the summer in Yellowstone.

Their group drifted out in ones and twos, attracted by R.J.'s sign. Hal checked them off while R.J. directed them outside to the bus with their luggage.

Half an hour later, they'd accounted for everyone apart from Corey Wilson.

Hal scanned the new arrivals. "Did any of you meet Corey during the flight?"

"There was one other guy," a girl offered. "He stopped to chat up the flight attendant when we deplaned."

R.J. groaned. The worst part of his job was avoiding cross-pollination, as Hal jokingly referred to it, of male and female students. He needed an extra set of eyes and the energy to keep three steps ahead of the horny teenagers. Thanks to some forward planning by the committee who remembered their younger days, anti-pregnancy drugs were mandatory, but R.J. still hated the chaperone part of the job.

"Damn," Hal muttered. "They don't usually focus on sex until the novelty of Yellowstone wears off."

A derisive snort erupted from R.J. "This kid *is* older."

"More advanced. That's all we need," Hal said in an undertone.

The double doors slid open and a young male sauntered

through.

"Fuck."

R.J. blinked, totally in charity with his boss. With a bemused shake of his head, he strode over to the male. "Corey Wilson?"

"Yeah." The kid's tone resonated with swagger and attitude.

R.J. struggled to maintain a neutral expression. Corey Wilson wore black—everything from the tight T-shirt to the leather jacket, jeans and biker boots. His long hair hung in lank strands, unnaturally black and harsh against his pale cheeks. Black eyeliner outlined his brown eyes. And...R.J. thought the kid wore mascara. There was no doubt about the black lipstick. The knowing smile on those painted lips finally jerked R.J. back to professional.

It took him a second or two longer to realize Corey returned his scrutiny with equal intensity and to register the interest flaring in the kid's face.

Sexual curiosity.

R.J. took in Corey's muscular thighs and broad chest. Not such a kid, despite the air of city softness. Corey Wilson was an adult and his face bore frank awareness of R.J. He offered his hand and R.J. stared, off balance and at a disadvantage. No one—man or woman—ever surveyed him with such blatant lust.

"My father informed me I'd find things different out here, but I'm sure he told me this was the place to learn manners." Silent laughter trembled in the words, yanking R.J. from his trance. He extended his hand, his callused palm meeting snow-white skin. He grasped the kid's hand and shook it, tempering his strength.

The firm grip dragged his glance to Corey's fingers. "You're wearing nail polish."

"There's a law against painted nails?" Corey's quizzical smile offered a glimpse of startling white teeth.

R.J.'s eyes narrowed. Not only did the kid dress like a Goth, but he bore a smart attitude, which didn't bode well for the next three months. "Come and help me load your luggage. We're keeping everyone waiting."

"Can't have that." Corey's lips curved into a genuine smile, the expression taking him from smart-ass, weird Goth to another beast entirely.

R.J. jolted from his sensual haze. Fuck! Hal was right. This kid spelled trouble and unfortunately he'd scored the job of babysitter.

"Here's my luggage." Corey indicated a man pushing a trolley laden with bags.

R.J. studied the four matching black bags. Expensive designer luggage. "All of it?"

"Yeah, I wanted to make sure I came prepared for every

eventuality."

R.J. gave a clipped nod, starting to gain an inkling of why Corey Wilson's family wanted to ship him here for the summer. The kid—man—was trouble waiting to happen. An ache sprang to life at his temples, its nagging presence hovering like a stormy cloud.

"Can you grab two and I'll take the others?"

Corey waggled his painted nails in front of R.J. "I'd hate to chip my nail polish. Is that our bus? I'll wait with the others." He sauntered away without a backward glance, leaving R.J. to tip the porter and load the bags. Realizing his mouth hung open, R.J. growled under his breath and wrestled with the oversized bags, trying to cram them into the luggage compartment. No problem. He'd have his subtle revenge and soon. Like the rest of the group, Corey Wilson would share a cabin and, with space at a premium, he'd have to pare down his belongings or sleep outdoors. None of the city kids took well to living rough at first. R.J. couldn't envision the bags filling up cabin space for long.

One glimpse of the stern man wearing the Yellowstone polo shirt and faded jeans and Corey's heart, the traitorous organ, jerked into a pitter-patter jig of excitement. Oh, he'd imagined himself in lust before but never like this—a punch to the gut and breath-stealing desire tracking straight to his cock. Despite his stern face and the quickly veiled shock, the guy rated extra hot on the hawt scale.

Tall and muscular. His short dark hair showed off the strong planes of his face. Intense gray eyes flashed a sexy glare each time they focused on him. His mouth...well, a set of full lips like his weren't for mere kissing. They'd stretch perfectly around a cock. Without warning, Corey craved a sight of R.J. on his knees, mouth wrapped around *his* dick.

Yeah, in the near future he'd make his fantasies real.

Somehow.

After all, a challenge provided a fun way of spicing up life.

He glanced away, intuition telling him the sexy man stared after him. The temptation to twitch his butt pulled at him. He resisted, not wanting to overplay his hand. The anticipation of the chase was part of the fun. There'd be plenty of time for seduction since his parents' wishes put him in this no-town dump for the next three months.

A scowl burst to life at the reminder. Who the hell wanted to run around in a fur coat anyway? The memory of the pain and sheer savagery of shifting to wolf form brought a shudder of horror. Shoving the past away, he boarded the yellow bus and took possession of an empty seat. He'd noticed the others on the plane. They'd taken one peek at him and judged by appearance, deeming his Goth makeup and apparel weird. A couple of the girls had treated him as if he carried cooties. A huff of contempt layered with humor escaped. Little did they know they were safe from his lecherous ways.

The males—now that was another matter entirely.

Park Ranger Cutie stowed the last of the bags in the compartment at the rear of the bus. From where he sat, Corey watched him surreptitiously, appreciating the smooth flex and bulge of biceps each time he hefted a bag from the luggage trolley. Giggling from two of the girls told Corey he wasn't the sole audience of this show. The girls were out of luck, however, because judging by the flicker of awareness he'd witnessed earlier, he stood a better chance of scoring. If he wasn't mistaken, Park Ranger Cutie preferred men, which suited Corey fine.

An older man boarded the bus, clipboard in hand. Park Ranger Cutie took possession of the driver's seat.

"Welcome to Yellowstone. I'm Hal Price-Jones, the director of the summer program. R.J. Blake here is our driver. He's my second-in-command and the person you'll come into contact with most on a day-to-day basis. We'll have a meeting tonight after dinner where R.J. and I will go through the rules and schedule. Our program will start officially tomorrow."

R.J. Blake lifted a hand in acknowledgment and turned away to start the bus. Corey pulled his sunglasses from his shirt pocket, placed them on and sprawled back in his seat. Most people would assume him asleep and leave him alone.

His thoughts drifted. Nine months ago his parents had informed him he'd spend his summer in Yellowstone. They expected him to ignore his art and learn to turn furry, enabling them to concentrate on consolidation with a neighboring pack. He'd tried objecting, promising to keep a low profile. His father said he was a smart-ass and he didn't trust him to behave in a manner befitting a pack leader's son. The consolidation was important and nothing could derail the talks. Nothing.

When calm reasoning failed, Corey had rebelled worse than usual. During full moon, when the call to shift pulled stronger than normal, his rage at his father's edicts fucked with his control. The infallible suppression drugs failed to hold him to human form and he'd partially shifted.

Corey fidgeted on the hard seat. Sweat beaded on his brow as his mind skittered through the terror again. The scrunching sounds. The musky scent of wolf. The agony when his bones and muscles warred with his mind. His gut roiled, the memories pounding him like a giant metal mallet. No wonder he lacked enthusiasm for this Yellowstone experience. Each nightmare replayed the shitload of pain.

Bad enough hiding in the gay closet, but having a resident wolf writhing inside him sucked great big donkey's balls.

Someone tapped him on the back. Corey ignored the interruption until the person grasped his shoulder and yanked insistently.

"What do you want?" Corey demanded.

"Aren't you looking forward to the next three months?" a breathless feminine voice asked.

Great. Just great. "I didn't want to come. My father decided to send me here as punishment." Corey opened his eyes, part of him curious. His appearance normally put off people.

"Ooh, what did you do?" The breathless voice belonged to a vivacious blonde. Her clothes screamed popular cheerleader. Perkiness seeped out of her pores in puke-inducing waves.

"Did you break a pack law? Why is your father punishing you? All my friends applied to attend. They were pissed when they missed out." Her redhead friend sat beside her like a matching bookend, apart from the hair color.

Corey inspected his fingernails for chipped polish before deigning to reply. Not too bad. The nail polish cost heaps but possessed great staying power. "According to my father, I'm an embarrassment."

The two cheerleaders leaned forward, their blue eyes rounding in fascination. "Why? What did you do?"

"I like art. My father thinks it's sissy." Luckily none of the pack was aware of his preference for the male sex. The discovery would likely get him kicked out of the pack. The two teens craned forward even farther. Most guys would have taken the opportunity to peer down their blouses. Corey wasn't that guy. "Also I don't play nice." He peeled back his lips to display sharp teeth. "I eat little girls like you for dinner."

They giggled.

"That's what we thought," the blonde whispered, glancing over her shoulder to learn if any of the others were eavesdropping.

Corey rolled his eyes. The drugs didn't kill their senses, merely muted them and stole their ability to shift. They were frickin' werewolves. Of course they were listening.

"We're best friends." She lowered her voice. "We do everything together. *Everything*." She blew him a kiss while her redhead friend winked at him.

Christ in a camper van. They wanted a threesome. With

him. His wolf stirred. Oh hell. Not now! He sucked in a breath through his mouth and concentrated on his current painting, recreating each brushstroke in his mind.

"Are you okay?" one of the girls asked.

"Yeah. I...ah...get motion sickness sometimes."

"I'll open the window," one of the girls said. "The fresh air always helps me."

"Thanks." Finally his wolf subsided, and wrung out, Corey slumped lower on the seat.

"Better?"

"Yeah. Thanks." What the hell would happen once he stopped taking the drugs? The possible answers scared him.

The unknown.

His father really would disown him if he caused the pack embarrassment, and his problems would increase because the drugs didn't stop wolves craving the company of like. No matter how much he fought the desire, eventually his inner wolf drove him crazy and he had to return to visit his parents and the rest of the pack. A sort of a recharge because his wolf only rested easy when he had frequent contact with other werewolves.

"So what do you think?" Both girls beamed at him, fluttering their eyelashes in well rehearsed flirtation.

"I'll keep your offer in mind." *Heck no. Never.* Corey

wouldn't touch them even if they paraded naked in front of him. The warning on the director's face when he glowered over his shoulder at them proved unnecessary. "I'm tired. I'm going to sleep." He turned away and pretended to nap. Art. He needed to concentrate on his artwork because if he didn't, his wolf would push him again, despite the suppression pills.

Gah! How the heck was he gonna survive the next three months?

No way, no how did he want to end up in between wolf and human again. His half state had intrigued the pack medical staff, but he could do without a repeat of the excruciating pain.

He must have fallen asleep in truth because the bus stopped. Corey sat up and inhaled, employing the wolfish senses he loathed to determine their location. Through the open window he caught a whiff of dried grass, pine trees, and the rich aroma of earth tinged with manure. The strong stench of human threatened to overpower nature—sweat battling with the sweetness of floral perfumes and soaps. Corey's nose twitched and a sneeze erupted.

The door to the bus shuddered open and Hal stood, pausing to grab his clipboard. "Give me a minute to get organized and I'll allocate your cabins as you exit the bus.

R.J. will unload the luggage. Please collect your bags once you have your cabin number. Dinner is at six-thirty sharp. We'll go through the rules and activities for the next week after we've finished our meal. Any questions?"

No one uttered a word, Corey included. Oh, the temptation tugged at him to make a smart-ass comment but, as Gerald, his art gallery boss, had reminded him during one of his many rants, this holiday gave him an opportunity to draw and record some of the flora and fauna. He hadn't liked to ask Gerald how he'd lug his art supplies around Yellowstone while in wolf form. Despite his broad mind, Gerald wasn't ready to learn of the beasts inhabiting the city.

None of the humans were, hence the rabid need for secrecy and the suppression drugs. Humans would certainly descend into panic if they discovered their beloved president held a secret—the ability to shift into a werewolf.

Corey waited his turn to alight from the bus. The two cheerleaders peeked at him over their shoulders, fluttered their eyelashes again and giggled. He muttered a soft curse.

"Corey, you're in cabin six," Hal said.

Corey nodded and went to collect the two of his bags containing art supplies. "I'm in cabin six. Bring my other two bags." The glare from Park Ranger Cutie jump-started

Corey's pulse. He drew a sharp breath to settle his wolf again. There was no point in letting R.J. learn of his attraction too quickly. He'd prefer a subtle game. First off, he needed to discover if R.J. was one of his father's friends. A friendship with his father, unfortunately, would make him out of bounds.

"You want your bags, you come back and get them." R.J.'s harsh, growling tone slid across Corey's nerve endings with delicious friction. Blood flowed to his dick, but Corey merely smirked and kept walking, following the directional signs to his cabin.

The door stood wide open when he arrived. He clattered up the two wooden steps leading inside and came to a halt in the doorway. His three roommates had already chosen their beds and stowed their bags. He claimed the last remaining spot—the top bunk nearest the door.

"Hey." Corey scanned the storage area. There wasn't much space for their bags.

The three stared at him, scrutinizing his makeup and sniggering.

"Do your parents let you go out like that?" one asked.

Corey shrugged. "I'm over twenty-one. They can't make me do anything." Apart from withholding funds until he was forced to follow their instructions, and putting up obstacles to get in his way. Of course, he could tell them to go jump, and find a better job, but he loved the art gallery. He refused to do without art, which meant he followed his parents' rules for the most part.

The cabin was small with not much more than the two sets of bunk beds and a scarred wooden table. He placed a bag on top of the table, making it wobble sharply to the left. He grabbed his bag before it toppled to the ground.

A small pot-bellied stove took up one corner, its presence attesting to the coldness of the winter. Logs of wood filled the cane basket sitting alongside. Surely the temperatures didn't get cold enough for fires up here during the middle of summer?

"Man, I'm looking forward to this summer. I can't wait to ditch the drugs and run in wolf form. I'm John," he added.

"Scott," a short, dark-haired boy said.

"Teague," the tallest and biggest of the three said. He scowled at Corey. "You'd better not snore."

"No one has complained before."

A thump on the door made them jump. They turned to see R.J. filling the doorway. "You," he said, jerking his thumb in a gesture at Corey. "Your bags are blocking the bus."

"Why didn't you bring them with you?" Corey wallowed in the burst of attraction. R.J. sure smelled good.

"I'm not here to wait on you. If your bags aren't moved by the time I'm ready to shift the bus, I'll back over them."

"Okay. I'll come and get them now." Corey stepped through the doorway and purposely brushed against the older man. He savored the quick rush of lust and the heat coming off R.J.'s body. A second hit of the man's scent didn't hurt either. He greedily dragged the smell into his lungs, trying to decipher the exact origin. Their gazes met for a second, held, and in that moment Corey knew he'd found what he was looking for. Oh, yeah. There was no doubt about it. He wanted this intriguing steely man like a chubby kid wanted a second piece of cake.

Chapter Two

R.J. REGISTERED THE INSTANT the kid made a decision. His gut cinched tight at the recognition, but he couldn't dispute the attraction simmering inside him. Something about Corey snared his interest. A city kid for God's sake. They had nothing in common. He eyed the tight black jeans practically painted on the kid's shapely ass. His gaze wandered higher, taking in the broad shoulders and surprisingly muscular chest, given Corey's pale skin indicated he preferred to spend his time indoors.

At almost twenty-two, he was bigger and bulkier than the others. It was difficult to decipher his natural looks under the layers of makeup. R.J. shook his head in bemusement.

Lipstick, and black at that.

The urge to drag the kid behind the nearest pine tree and lay one on him brought edginess and irritation. A single kiss, so he could tell himself they wouldn't suit and this urge was his body's way of prompting him to make a trip to town. Yeah. On his next weekend off, he'd go to Cody. Maybe find himself a hot cowboy at the Cody Nite Rodeo and fuck the willing man into oblivion before returning to Yellowstone.

The kid fell into step with him. R.J. didn't like the way his wolf came to attention, stretching under his skin as if waking from a long slumber. He'd gone hunting only last night. His wolf should rest peacefully, but instead he stirred because of Corey.

Thinking about a kiss was a bad, bad idea.

"What do you do for entertainment around here?" Corey asked.

"I don't get much time off during the summer while we're running camps."

"But you must get some time off. What do you do then?"

"I go hunting." R.J. wasn't about share the fact he did his hunting in pubs and clubs. He went out to meet willing men.

"What if you want to get laid?"

R.J.'s wolf jolted at the punch of heat that struck him.

"I go to the bar and find a willing woman."

"A woman?"

R.J. wanted to laugh at the kid's obvious disappointment. If experience had taught him something, it was how to lie convincingly. "Our equipment works well together."

"Male equipment works with either sex," the kid retorted with a sidelong glance at R.J.'s groin.

R.J. willed his body not to react, even though Corey's attention sent more heat skipping through his veins. "Move it, kid. I have lots to do before dinner."

"I'm not a kid."

Yeah, R.J. agreed with the assessment, which made Corey a problem for him. He'd always allowed himself to follow up on an attraction. This time he couldn't. Taking advantage of one of their charges wasn't appropriate. Besides, the kid's father held a position of importance in the L.A. pack. No way did R.J. want to attract attention and have suppression drugs forced on him again. No, he preferred to keep under the radar and enjoy his life here at Yellowstone. He focused on puncturing Corey's smirk. "You're a kid to me."

"Do you know my father?"

"Are you trying to threaten me?"

"No, it was a simple question. Do you know my father?"

"I've never met him." Thank goodness, by all accounts. R.J. turned away to head for his bus, confident of handling his attraction to the kid. He'd be too busy to indulge his desires anyway.

The orientation meeting started with Hal running through the rules. "You will follow every direction issued by either me or R.J. This is for your safety." He paused to scan the kids. "There will be no sneaking into the cabins of the opposite sex. R.J. will make bed checks every night."

R.J. hid his amusement when he saw the consternation on a couple of faces.

"Everyone will have a chore assignment. You'll take turns to help with meals and the cleanup afterward." Hal nodded at him.

R.J. took over. "We're going to wean you off the suppression drugs gradually and help you learn the skills to control your wolves before the drug leaves your systems. We will teach you to track and read your surroundings using all your senses. At the end of the month, we'll start camping out overnight. The goal of the program is to get back to nature and to embrace your wolves. At the end of the three months we expect you to each make a kill."

"We have to kill an animal?" The young girl gaped at him

in disbelief.

Hal glanced at R.J., silently indicating he should jump into the conversation again before mass hysteria erupted.

"Making a kill is a natural thing and part of nature's controls," R.J. said. "The game populations swell to unnatural numbers if the regular cycle isn't adhered to. It's a fine balance."

Another one of the girls raised her hand. "You mean we have to kill a Bambi?" Her voice rose to a squeak toward the end of her sentence.

"Killing prey to eat is a natural thing," R.J. repeated in a firm voice before any of the other eleven kids offered their opinion. "There will be no discussion. Your parents have paid us to give you this experience."

"Any other questions?" Hal scanned their faces and waited.

Corey put up his hand. "Yeah, what can we do in our free time? Are we allowed to leave the camp?"

"You can join in with any of the park activities," R.J. said. "You're free to interact with humans, keeping in mind they aren't aware of the existence of werewolves. If you wish to leave the camp area for any reason, you must tell either me or Hal. No alcohol allowed since you're under age. If we catch a whiff of alcohol, we'll kick you out of the program. No second chances. This is the only warning you'll receive."

"I'm legal." Corey leaned back on his chair until the front legs left the ground. "I'm an adult."

R.J. met his challenging stare. "Act like a mature adult and I might believe you." Instead of arguing, the kid scrutinized him thoughtfully before nodding. The tacit agreement should've reassured R.J., but instead an alarm fired to life. The kid's attitude implied he liked to flout convention rather than follow along with everyone else. Not that R.J. could do much about his mind-set. No. He'd impose the camp rules and take appropriate action if or when any of the kids broke one.

He shoved his trepidation aside. "Any more questions? No? Good. Hal will pin the chore roster on the notice board in a few minutes. We'll split you into two groups and start your training tomorrow. Meantime, I want you to collect the correct dosage pills from me before you leave."

R.J. dispensed the pills, ticking off names as the kids received their tablets. The last one to receive medication was Corey. Of course.

"Where do you go to get a drink around here?" The kid's eyes gleamed with challenge, and R.J. found himself wanting to grin. The makeup didn't bother him now that he'd become used to the startling effect of stark black against Corey's pale skin. He stared a fraction longer, and when he wondered what Corey looked like without the makeup, he admitted the kid had reeled him in like a curious trout.

"We told you earlier, you don't get a drink around here."

Corey clicked his fingers. "Well damn. I'll have to settle for sex."

The minute the kid mentioned sex, the vague element of trouble rumbling in R.J.'s gut solidified. He forced himself not to react to Corey's smirk. Instead, he stared at Corey's mouth. Normally sexual attraction came and went. Sex was like scratching an itch—a momentary thing he took care of when the need arose. This weird...fascination...had struck without warning, pouncing out at him.

Aware of Corey's amusement, R.J. forced his mind back to business. He couldn't let the kid rattle him. "Take the blue pill tonight and the pink pill tomorrow night. The medication will ease you down and help you keep better control of your wolf until Hal and I can run through some exercises and give you more information tomorrow."

Corey nodded. "Blue then pink. Got it. You didn't answer my question."

"You didn't ask a question." R.J. cursed silently. Talking about sex with Corey Wilson wouldn't help keep his mind straight.

Corey glanced over his shoulder, confirmed they were

alone and leaned closer. "I'd like to have sex with you."

His words hung between them, inherent with promise. R.J. wanted to turn away and couldn't. The kid didn't mince words. No, like any good wolf he went for the throat.

"You can't say that."

Corey's too-black brows rose. "Why?"

"It's inappropriate."

"But not impossible," Corey countered. "See you tomorrow."

He strode away with a real swagger, leaving R.J. staring after him in consternation.

"Something wrong?" Hal returned from the kitchen and came to a halt beside R.J.

"No. This intake of kids seems like a good group." A lie, but if all else failed, denying everything worked for him. Corey Wilson was a problem waiting to happen.

THE NEXT MORNING, R.J. mentally checked off the kids' names against the list he'd memorized. Everyone was present apart from Corey Wilson.

"Has anyone seen Corey?"

One of the guys paused, his spoon of cereal hovering in

front of his mouth. "He was still in bed when we left the cabin. Said he didn't do breakfast and would catch some extra zees."

Still in bed. Figured. R.J. cursed under his breath. He did *not* need a mental visual of Corey plus a bed stuck in his head.

"Finish your breakfast. I want you outside, waiting near the bus, in fifteen minutes with your day packs. Grab a packed lunch from outside the kitchen before you leave. They're all the same. And don't forget to bring your water bottle. Make sure it's full because by the time we're finished with you you're gonna need the water."

R.J. left the dining hall and made for cabin six. The door stood closed when he arrived. He sniffed, letting the restraint on his wolf loosen while he scented the air. He caught the distinct scent of pack, which he expected since the pills they gave the kids contained chemicals to make them smell alike. He twisted the doorknob and pushed the door hard enough to smack it against the wall. The crack of wood echoed in the small cabin. Only the top bunk nearest him contained an occupant. One pale leg stuck out from beneath a white sheet.

"Corey," he barked. The urge to raise the sheet, to touch bare skin, whispered at him. It was his healthy libido. The impulse was nothing to do with his inappropriate attraction for the kid. "Corey, wake up."

Nothing happened. A couple of young girls strutted past, curiosity burning in their faces. Cursing softly, R.J. stepped into the room and shut the door after him. He grabbed Corey's shoulder and shook.

The kid's eyes popped open. Sexy brown. They stared at each other. Corey's face held the softness of youth still, his skin pale like pristine winter snow. The coming days, spent outdoors, would leave their stamp on him.

"Hey," Corey said, his face open and full of yearning. Distinct sexual hunger.

R.J. backed up a step, both hands tightened to fists at his sides. He forced himself to remain where he stood, while inside he trembled with the yen to touch Corey again, to stroke and explore the tender skin.

Hell! R.J. mentally shook himself and retreated even farther from temptation. "Everyone is waiting for you."

"I'd better get moving." Corey flung the sheet off and slid down from the top bunk in a quick graceful move that had R.J. blinking. "Care to help me out here?" His grin widened as he gestured at his morning wood.

R.J. recoiled, the hard wall at his back halting his retreat. Hell, he was the one in charge here. "Meet the rest of us out front in five minutes. Bring your day pack and a full water bottle. Collect your lunch from the kitchen."

"Five minutes? But I have to shower and put on my makeup first."

"Five minutes or we go without you."

Corey's chin shot upward. "I didn't want to come here. It's no skin off my nose if you leave me behind."

"Let me rephrase." R.J. straightened, carefully keeping his gaze on Corey's face instead of sightseeing. "If you're not waiting with the rest of the kids within the five minutes, I will drag you to the bus myself." He backed up his threat with a glare before he left.

Three steps from the cabin he let his breath ease out. There was nothing kidlike about Corey Wilson. Sweet Jesus, he'd tried not to stare, but the one quick glimpse he'd managed had seared his retinas. He wouldn't have difficulty recalling Corey's body in the future.

Most of the kids loitered around the bus when R.J. reached the meeting point. The girls chattered together like noisy birds, and it wasn't difficult to spot the flirtatious moves taking place between several of the youngsters. R.J.'s mouth set, even though an evil grin wanted to take possession. By the time he finished with them today they'd be dog-tired, too exhausted to do anything except fall onto their bunk beds.

"Okay, everyone on the bus. Have you packed your water bottles?"

A chorus of affirmations greeted him.

"I'll return once I grab my day pack and lunch." R.J. jogged around the front of the bus and came face-to-face with Corey. He wore his pack slung over his shoulder and his face was makeup free. Although he'd donned black clothes again, the view was one hundred percent better than yesterday.

"Looking good, kid." As soon as he uttered the words, R.J. grimaced. *Big mouth.* Corey didn't need that sort of encouragement. Fuck, he had no idea what drew him to Corey, but this crazy behavior had to stop.

"Everyone ready?" Hal asked, falling into step with R.J.

"Yeah. I'm collecting my lunch." Hurried steps behind him made him turn. Corey. Of course. "Where are you going?"

Corey grinned. "I'm gonna grab something to eat before we head out."

"Breakfast is finished," R.J. said firmly. "If you miss a meal, that's your problem. The kitchen staff aren't here to cater for individuals. Do you have your lunch pack?"

"Yes, but I haven't—"

R.J. nailed Corey with such a fierce glare the kid pulled up short and took half a step back. "Everyone else managed to rise in time for breakfast. Think about that while you're waiting on the bus." He waited for Corey to argue, part of him amazed when he didn't. To his surprise Corey gave a curt nod, wheeled around and headed to the bus.

Hal barked out a short laugh. "I didn't see that coming. I thought he'd argue."

R.J. ripped his gaze off Corey's ass and rubbed his face. "Yeah. Stunned me too. Do you have a lunch package? Should I get you one?"

A feminine shriek came from the bus. "Good idea. I'll go and calm the restless natives."

They parted company, and five minutes later, R.J. climbed behind the wheel and started the bus. He aimed the vehicle in the direction he wanted, driving on automatic pilot. His pack held an extra lunch, and he still couldn't fathom why he'd retraced his steps and grabbed another one for Corey. He scowled at the road, still perturbed by the impulsive action. When he'd told Corey to go without breakfast, he'd meant to teach him a valuable lesson.

In the wild, it was survival of the fittest. Each of the kids needed to take responsibility and own their actions. Corey needed to follow the rules. R.J. barely restrained a grunt of amusement. The kid took great pleasure in flouting convention.

R.J. slowed and came to a halt behind a line of cars, waiting for a herd of bison to meander across the road. As usual, a couple of dumb-ass tourists parked haphazardly, intent on approaching the animals, stalking them with digital cameras in hand. They wanted a souvenir picture to show the folks back home. *Idiots*.

"See those people over there," R.J. called out.

"Yeah," a few of the kids replied.

"They're setting an example of what not to do with bison. The herd might appear slow and friendly, but they move fast if the desire strikes them. If they're in the mood they can also take exception to vehicles."

"I'll show you a couple of film clips after dinner tonight," Hal added. "You'll view footage of what happens when people get too close."

"Does that mean we shouldn't choose a bison when we come to make our kill?"

Corey, of course. Corey would have a smart-ass question. R.J. clenched his hands around the steering wheel, blood rushing south where it had no business heading. The kid made him think about sex way too much.

Hal turned in his seat to answer their questions. "Wolves can take down a bison, but normally we'd work in a team, cutting the beast off from the herd and running it into the ground. We'd always choose a calf or an animal displaying weakness. One that's injured."

"Most likely your kill will be an elk or some sort of deer.

Maybe a pronghorn." R.J. inched the bus forward when the traffic started to move.

"They're so big," Corey said.

A jolt of lust hit his body at the husky note in the kid's voice. R.J. focused fiercely on the traffic in front of the bus. He refused to let his mind consider other big things. Oh, wait. His cock was way ahead of him. R.J. struggled to check his unruly body and started to recite the different states of America.

"They're ugly," one of the girls said.

"Ooh!" another girl said. "Look at the baby one. Isn't he cute?"

"They're dangerous," Hal said. "They might appear cuddly, but don't ever take them for granted."

Finally the line of traffic moved freely again. R.J. trailed the other vehicles until he came to a turnoff to a hiking trail. The kids peppered them with questions about the various animals they might observe and the places they'd explore. A sense of satisfaction filled R.J. when Corey joined the conversation with the others.

Hawaii. Alaska. Nevada. New Mexico. He mentally listed the states and let out a sigh of relief when his cock relaxed. Yeah, he could rein in the attraction, and control would become even easier once Corey made friends. Yellowstone never failed to work magic on visitors, and the more they interacted with others and discovered nature, the simpler his job would become.

R.J. drove to the end of the tarmac and parked the bus.

"This is it," Hal said. "We're going to split into two groups here. Six of you will go with R.J. and six with me. Make sure you have your lunch and water bottle."

Once everyone alighted from the bus, R.J. grabbed his pack and locked up. Shrugging his pack over one shoulder, he joined the others.

"This group can go with R.J.," Hal said. "The rest of you come with me." He departed down the trail, leaving five eager teenagers plus Corey with R.J.

R.J. scanned the faces. Quick with names, he ran through his group. Two bubbly cheerleader types, Beth and Maria; Corey's roomies, Teague—the scholarship boy—plus John and Scott.

"Okay, listen up. Others use this trail and we don't want them to overhear things they shouldn't." Mentor-mode. "Did everyone take their pills this morning?" Something he should have checked before they left their base.

All the kids nodded except Corey.

"I forgot."

Hell. "Do you feel okay?" The last thing R.J. wanted to deal with was an out-of-control wolf. The need to work within the constraints of the park and the human tourists was the reason they weaned the kids off the drugs. They required time to learn control and to deal with their heightened senses.

Corey paused, considering his answer. "I think so. Everything seems more...sort of enhanced." He lifted his head and tested the wind. "My smell and sight is sharper than normal."

"You should all experience enhanced senses during the coming days." R.J. glanced around the circle of faces. Young faces, he reminded himself when his gaze settled on Corey's visage. He appeared unusually serious, brown eyes full of emotions as he studied their surroundings. Pleasure slid across his features. That's what he'd look like when he had sex...

Ohio. California. Washington. R.J. jerked his gaze away to focus on the two girls in the group. "What can you smell?"

The kids fell silent and tested the air with intent expressions on their young faces.

"The different plants," one of the girls replied. "They have a strong scent, more pungent than the ones in the city park at home."

"The dirt," the other girl said.

Teague grinned in triumph. "Animal droppings."

"Perfume," Corey said.

"I can hear people," Scott said, after they'd taken stock of their surroundings again. "Arguing."

R.J. nodded in approval. "A family group is heading down the trail toward us." He'd no sooner finished his sentence than four people—two adults plus two children—came into view on the track ahead of them. All were dressed casually in shorts and T-shirts, and footwear unsuitable for tackling the terrain. Their faces were flushed red with exertion. Sweat shone on their brows. R.J. stood back for them to pass. "Did you see anything interesting on the trail?"

"Nothing," the father said in disgust. "Not a single animal. What a waste of an hour." They continued past, talking in loud voices, a wave of chemical perfume wafting in their wake.

R.J. waited until they'd disappeared into their campervan. "They didn't catch a glimpse of any wildlife because they spoke in loud voices, and you might have noticed their scent. Any sensible animal hid the instant they sensed them. If you want to see animals, you must move silently and blend with the surroundings. The same is true when you're in wolf form. If I'm hunting, I'll sometimes roll on the grass or rub up against the bushes to disguise my scent." His gaze slid to Corey. "Corey, if you start to feel strange I want you to tell me immediately.

37

Stopping the suppression drugs abruptly can mess with you.

"We're going to take the trail to the summit of this peak and we'll take a break there for our lunch. It's not a race. We'll pace ourselves and will stop regularly. Questions?" He noted their anticipation with approval. Succumbing to Yellowstone's charms didn't take long, and the transformation never failed to give him a sense of satisfaction.

"What if we get tired?" Beth asked. "I'm not very fit."

"I'll carry you," Teague said, waggling his eyebrows to comic effect.

"We all will," John said.

"You just want to cop a feel," Beth said.

"Yep," Teague agreed while the others hooted with laughter.

"Let's go." R.J. cut through the flirting and took the lead. The fresh air and sunshine soon lightened his mood. The tenseness in his shoulders faded. Hal and this job had saved his sanity, made him whole again after his parents' deaths and the lingering horror of their massacre. Whenever Corey tempted him he needed to remember his job and the security it provided him. The loss of his job and purpose would leave a huge hole in his life.

Corey tailed the group, taking in the trees and other surroundings with pleasure. He'd fought coming to Yellowstone, protested bitterly to his father, his mother and anyone who'd listen to him. The camp was okay and nothing like the prison he'd conjured in his imagination. The sights, the smells. The colors of Yellowstone. They spoke to the artist in him. His fingers literally itched to capture what he saw on paper. His steps slowed and he wished he'd remembered to bring his camera. It was still at the cabin because he'd hurried this morning and had forgotten to grab it.

"Corey." The abrupt bark jerked him to the present.

R.J. stood in the middle of the trail, waiting for him. Six-foot plus of impatient male.

Something about the man brought a flash of anxiety, and excuses sprang to his lips. "I stopped to tie my shoe lace." He was big, so sure of himself and his place in the world. And attractive. Sexy. Right now Corey would offer his left nut for permission to lift R.J.'s tight blue T-shirt and touch his muscled chest.

"Keep up. I don't want to waste my time searching for you." He waited for Corey to reach him and once he'd passed, R.J. walked behind him.

The sensation of R.J. at his back ripped his mind off

the grassy meadow and the trees. Like a spotlight, every one of his brain cells focused on R.J.'s presence. He smelled the man's scent, heard his soft breaths and the rustle of his clothing. Blood flowed thickly through his veins, flooding his cock. His shaft lengthened, swelled, and walking became uncomfortable, every step sensual torture. Yeah, it was like persecution because Corey wasn't used to denying himself anything. In the sexual arena, if something felt good, he embraced the activity.

Heck, he needed to entice R.J. into touching him in a sexual way or he'd go crazy before the end of three months.

The morning passed rapidly, with frequent stops for R.J. to tell them about the plant or animal life they discovered or to offer them another snippet of advice about embracing their wolf.

The longer they hiked, the more excitement pulsed through Corey. If he'd known Yellowstone would be like this he wouldn't have argued about taking the trip. He scanned the trees and scrubby bushes, the views over the plains, every one of his senses working on overload. Lightheaded, he felt almost drunk on the rush of smells and sights, his enhanced hearing. Even the brush of foliage against his bare arm brought a thrill of awareness.

In the city, the smells were often noxious and the sight of a beggar at the street corner didn't make his heart race like a glimpse of a deer or a squirrel. The wilderness was a revelation, a life-changing experience even. A giddy laugh escaped. There was so much to see—the trees, the bushes, their leaves stirring a little in the breeze, the long grasses. Myriad scents crashed through his senses. The colors bombarded him. Green, everywhere he looked, in many different shades. In the past he'd concentrated on abstracts and cityscapes, some sculpture with metal and pieces of junk. He'd scoffed at artists who produced landscapes but no longer.

Now he comprehended their fervor and enthusiasm.

The sounds—they played through his mind like an orchestra. A cacophony of clicking and buzzing insects. There was the awkward clamber of the people as they scurried from sight to sight and the snap and zoom of their cameras. The songs played by the wind whispering through grasses, rustling the leaves. And the animals. To his right, a chattering chipmunk scolded them for venturing too close. A gasp of wonder escaped while he watched the tiny animal's antics.

"Corey! Keep up with the rest of us." R.J.'s exasperated tone finally jolted him from his trance, and he hastened his pace even as he noticed the man's quickly hidden amusement. Warmth suffused him because he sensed R.J. understood his rapture at his surroundings. Yeah, he'd protested leaving the city, calling it a life sentence. Now he wondered if three months would suffice to capture the wildlife experience in his art.

At the front of the line, R.J. halted abruptly, his attention on something deep in the undergrowth.

"What is it?" one of the girls asked.

"Quiet." R.J.'s hand gesture signaled them closer, his finger touching his lips indicating a need for silence.

Corey crept nearer with the others, his gaze scanning the dim shadows while anticipation hummed in him. Then he saw the creature. His eyes widened and his breath whooshed out with a faint hiss. A bear. A real live bear.

He dragged in the animal's scent, concentrating so he'd recognize the aroma in the future. The bear ceased its foraging, lifted its head and stared straight at them.

"Why doesn't he run away?" Corey asked in a low voice, secretly glad the bear hadn't retreated because he wouldn't have missed this for the world. Already he was trying to memorize the creature's lines and appearance, the exact color of its coat, to recreate on paper once they returned to camp.

"He doesn't have to run. The bear is high on the food chain here. It's probably confused because he can smell wolf but we're not in wolf form."

"What sort of bear is it?" Beth backed away with a

startled *eep* when the bear snorted.

"Grizzly. See the hump above its shoulders? That's how we distinguish between grizzly and black bears. Don't judge by color. Bears come in shades from blond to brown and black. Much like wolves," R.J. added.

Corey glanced at the others, observing the same enthrallment capturing him. Suddenly he couldn't wait to embrace his wolf, even though a sliver of fear lurked inside him. What happened if he managed to get stuck in a half-change again?

Frowning, he glanced at R.J. and found the big man staring. Corey winked, taking childish pleasure in the way color seeped into R.J.'s face, highlighting his cheekbones. Yeah, Yellowstone possessed lots of advantages he'd never considered before, including the sexy R.J. Blake.

With another sidelong glance, he checked on R.J. and caught him watching again. This time their gazes met and held. Instead of flirting or saying something suggestive, Corey smiled, letting his pleasure in the moment openly show. The man's gray eyes widened fractionally and he didn't crack a smile in return. It didn't matter. The reaction was enough for Corey. He'd been with men and spent enough time with others to sense R.J. returned his interest. R.J. could battle the attraction all he liked, but they'd end up together.

CHAPTER THREE

COREY'S BREATH CAUGHT AS they entered a high mountain meadow an hour later. The strenuous ascent of the steep track challenged all of them except R.J. With heaving sides and sweat glistening on his arms and legs, Corey stood beside the others, his thigh muscles quivering. Judging by the moans and groans from the others, they were suffering the same exhaustion.

Wildflowers peppered the green grass and the bubble of water indicated a small stream nearby. Something else for him to paint. Watercolors, maybe in an Impressionist style. Next time he wouldn't forget his camera. Whenever practical, he intended to take it with him to record the details his saturated mind would miss.

"We'll break for lunch here." R.J. shrugged his pack off

his broad shoulders, the play of muscles catching Corey's rapt attention. "Not many hikers come up here."

"Why not?" Maria asked, loosening her ponytail and recapturing stray blonde strands before fastening it again. "It's beautiful."

"Most people keep going to the summit. If they take this side trip, they can't get to the summit and back in one day, which most of them prefer to do."

"Their loss." Teague rolled his shoulders, letting out a husky groan. Although Corey witnessed the move, the sight didn't raise a blip on his sexual radar.

"I'm starving," John said.

The group removed their packs, Corey's belly rumbling with hunger once he heard the mention of food.

"We'll set up camp farther away from the trailhead, in case we get human visitors." R.J. led the way over to the far side of the meadow, and Corey found himself dawdling, the last to reach their picnic spot, despite his gnawing hunger.

"When are you going to start telling us more about wolf stuff?" Scott asked. "When will we learn about shifting?"

"Yeah," Teague said. "When will we shift?"

Corey dropped his day pack on the ground and flopped onto the grass with a groan. His feet ached and his legs still quivered like jelly. They wouldn't be in so much of a hurry to shift if they knew how painful the process was and the horrid disorientation.

R.J. unzipped his pack and pulled out a packed lunch. "I'll start while we're eating."

Corey hurriedly followed suit, opening his lunch and sinking his teeth into the roast beef sandwich with a groan of pleasure. The meaty flavor exploded into his mouth. So good. Hell, he'd never tasted something this delicious in his entire life. He chewed rapidly and shoved half the remaining sandwich in his mouth, giving a soft growl of pleasure. He swallowed and grabbed a second one.

Someone was growling. He didn't bother looking, too intent on appeasing his hunger.

"Corey!"

Corey's head jerked up, eyes widening when he realized constant growls were issuing from his throat. He froze, and glanced down at his hands. A croak of shock escaped. Sharp claws poked from beneath his fingernails, like the time he'd made his half shift. His sandwich slipped from nerveless fingers, hitting the ground by his leg.

When another growl emerged, his fellow students backed away and Corey didn't blame them. Only R.J. moved closer, concern filling in his gray eyes.

"Corey, it's all right," R.J. said in a calm voice. "Don't fight your wolf. It's safe to change here. We're safe here. I won't let anyone hurt you."

Corey trembled, fear swelling to a hard ball in his gut. Somehow, his wolf had crept up on him, maybe because he was relaxed and happy for once, not trying to hide any facet of his identity—gayness or wolf.

A bolt of pain seared the length of his spine. He cried out, his limbs twitching painfully as his nerve endings reacted to the stimulus.

"Corey, strip." R.J. seized his shoulders to hold him in place, and yanked up the hem of his T-shirt. Normally Corey would make a smart-ass comment, but right now he couldn't raise the energy. Dread curled through him. He couldn't let this change happen. He'd end up transformed halfway, the pain enough to bring unmanly tears to his eyes. And the shame. His father hadn't spoken to him for weeks after the wolf medics had finished poking and prodding him, drawing his blood for medical tests. Becoming trapped in half form sucked, and he didn't want to experience it again.

R.J. rapidly unfastened Corey's jeans, jerking them down his legs until they reached his boots. "I'm going to talk you through the change. Are you listening? Corey?" R.J. kept talking, his voice soothing as he untied Corey's boot laces and removed his footwear.

"Yeah." His voice emerged in a guttural growl and the

harsh noise scared him even more. A sharp crack sounded and his jaw started to reshape. Agony writhed along his nerve paths, and his entire body jerked in a spasm. Corey swallowed and stared at his misshapen hand. Ugly coarse hair sprouted on the back. This hand couldn't hold a paintbrush or draw a line with a piece of charcoal. Horror writhed through him. Despair.

"Strip," R.J.'s persuasive tone propelled Corey into action. He met R.J.'s steady gaze, latched onto the connection and didn't let go, standing mutely while R.J. removed the last of his clothes. The fresh breeze played across his naked skin before the forceful push of his wolf sent him to his knees.

R.J. knelt at his side, whispering instructions. "Picture your wolf in your mind. Embrace him. Block out the pain of the shift. Concentrate, Corey. You can do this if you focus. I won't let anything happen to you. I promise."

"I don't know what my wolf looks like." Corey cringed at his harsh growl. How was he meant to know what his wolf looked like when shifting was illegal? Yeah, he'd partially shifted before but he didn't recall a good deal of the experience. He'd fainted at first.

Aware the other kids stared and murmured to each other, shame made him freeze. He'd embarrass himself and never manage to look them in the face again. A tremor racked his body. His father might actually carry out his threats and disown him if he screwed up again.

Whining softly, he continued to focus on R.J., the confident timbre of his voice going a long way to beat back Corey's panic.

"Picture your wolf. Do it. *Now*."

Corey attempted to speak, tried to tell R.J. he had no idea what his wolf looked like. A garbled growl emerged instead and that panicked him even more.

"Concentrate." R.J. spoke softly, rubbing his still-human shoulder in a comforting manner. "You can do this."

He homed in on R.J.'s confidence, the certainty in his demeanor. How did he know? Why was he so positive?

"I knew you were going to be the difficult one." Humor laced R.J.'s voice this time. "The troublemaker."

"Why is he changing? He took pills the same as us," Maria said, venturing closer.

"I'm not sure," R.J. said. "Although Corey forgot to take his pill this morning."

Beth tugged on the end of her ponytail. "Will the same thing happen to us?"

"No, this is the first time it's ever happened. The rest of you shouldn't experience the same problem as Corey."

"That's reassuring," Maria said dryly.

"I can't wait to embrace my wolf." Scott's voice held envy.

John high-fived him. "Yeah, shifting must have been great before the regulations governing the change came into force. I'm so glad the authorities decided to raise money for the presidential election this way."

Teague nodded. "Changing at will would be awesome."

Corey listened to their discussion closely. Their enthusiasm was an anchor for him to cling to while his bones and muscles twisted and reshaped. The discomfort forced another whimper from him. This was farther than he'd shifted before. Once he realized that, his tension eased. Fur rippled across the last of his exposed skin and his senses intensified a hundredfold, his vision fading to black and white and shades of gray.

Corey panted, crouching low, his belly to the grass. The pain torturing his nerves vanished. He was himself—Corey Wilson. He recalled every detail of his life, his likes and dislikes yet now there was more, every sensation he experienced multiplied.

"Good boy," R.J. said with approval. "You've done the hard part. Are you hungry?"

Corey understood everything, read the body language of the others in his group. His newfound knowledge was both exhilarating and scary at the same time.

"Corey? Are you hungry?"

Yes! Hunger filled him suddenly, his stomach rumbling and gurgling loud enough for the others to hear. He growled, remembering his remaining sandwich.

R.J. dug into his day pack and pulled out a second lunch packet. He opened it and extended the sandwich in Corey's direction.

Hunger took precedence. Corey snapped, his jaws closed around the sandwich and almost took off R.J.'s fingers in the process.

"Jesus, watch the fingers."

One of the girls chuckled and suddenly they were all laughing, even R.J.

"When can we shift like Corey?" Teague asked, a trace of envy coloring his words. "Man, I'm glad I worked so hard to get the scholarship to come here. It was worth every bit of effort."

Corey moved closer to R.J., pausing to read his reaction. R.J. cast him a sidelong glance, silently giving Corey permission to approach him. Corey crawled nearer until they almost touched.

"It's okay." R.J. reached out and ruffled the fur at the scruff of his neck, the rough gesture of acceptance filling Corey with quiet joy. He pressed closer still, arching his back when R.J. ran a hand down his spine.

Gradually Corey allowed himself to relax. His agitated heartbeat fell, resuming a more normal pace. He leaned into R.J. and the man never stopped his gentle, soothing caresses while he answered the questions the kids fired at him.

"Why didn't our families ever tell us any of this stuff?" John asked.

Yeah, exactly what Corey wanted to know. Why had the werewolf packs strayed so far from the old ways? He knew they wanted to keep the president in power, but why was it better to continually suppress their wolves?

"If our race is to survive we need to adapt and blend with everyone else," R.J. said. "In the past we lived in the wilderness and got on with our lives, running the pack in the old way. These days a lot of people have to move to the city for work because there's no work in the country. The wilderness areas are shrinking more each day."

Beth piped up, "And we can't have wolves shifting during the full moon. We would scare the humans."

"That's right." R.J. nodded, continuing to stroke Corey even though he no longer shivered. If anything, R.J.'s touch only confirmed to Corey his desire for the man. Electricity arced between them even if R.J. sought to deny the attraction. "Werewolves are strong and good leaders. We've reached positions of power in many governments.

The drugs help us to function in the human world without exposing ourselves."

"It would cost werewolves a lot of money if our secrets were revealed," Teague said.

True. People would lose money if humans discovered the truth and panicked, his father for example. No wonder he was so concerned about Corey's strong tolerance for the suppression drugs. His reputation was at stake.

"I don't understand why we have this camp if werewolves shifting is such a problem," Scott said.

"Not all wolves agreed with the new laws." R.J.'s fingers clenched his fur, tugging at it painfully. He cleared his throat and continued. "There was some concern that over the generations we would forget how to shift and perhaps mutate, losing the ability all together."

"I'm glad we have this opportunity," Teague said.

"It's rad," Scott said.

Even Beth and Maria nodded.

"Let's get back on track," R.J. said. "Take a look at Corey and paint a picture in your head of what a wolf looks like. I want you to practice whenever you think of it during the next two days. Practice deep breaths while holding the picture in your mind."

Corey tuned out. He hadn't considered coming off the pills would cause a problem. His mind had been more on the fact he would miss the advanced art course he'd wanted to attend. The whole purpose of the wilderness experience was to get back to nature and of course, make sure he didn't derail the pack consolidation at home. Since turning hairy was part of the plan, it hadn't occurred to him he'd morph quicker than the others. Obviously the risks hadn't occurred to his father either.

"But you don't take the drugs," one of the guys said.

"No, I don't like living in the city. Hal offered me a job here, and once I obtained the proper permit, I decided I liked the countryside better."

"Is it true they take the wolves who refuse to take the drugs into custody?" Maria asked.

"I don't know," R.J. replied. "I've heard rumors, but I haven't spoken to anyone who refused to take the drugs. Anyone who doesn't take the drugs must register with the central system and provide an iron-clad reason why they shouldn't take them."

Something in R.J.'s demeanor alerted Corey to the fact R.J. wasn't telling the truth. Did the Enforcers kill those who refused to take the drugs? A shiver seized him, and he pressed against R.J., silently seeking reassurance.

"Right, we're going to do some basic tracking. Corey will help me once we've finished eating."

Corey nudged R.J. with his nose, giving a soft

questioning whine.

"Don't worry. It's nothing difficult. I intend to teach you the basics of tracking, skills the older wolves used to teach but don't any longer because most of us don't need tracking while living in the city." As he spoke, R.J. unwrapped another lunch package, taking one sandwich for himself and giving one to Corey. This time Corey took the sandwich carefully. He forced himself to eat slowly and tried not to think about his wolf form, or even worse, what would happen if he couldn't change back.

R.J. handed Corey his last sandwich instead of eating it himself. He could deal with the hunger pangs. The kid needed the food more, strung out with shivers racking his body every time R.J. stopped petting him. Corey made a handsome wolf. He was a dark slate gray with none of the lighter variations most wolves bore these days. He wasn't big but a few more years would muscle him up further. He needed to stop stroking Corey yet couldn't seem to ignore the urge to touch him. Protective of the younger wolf, he couldn't refute the physical attraction even if he wanted to. Maybe if he focused on work and trained these youngsters to embrace their wolf, he'd manage to negate the attraction.

SHELLEY MUNRO

Yeah, and maybe werewolves would soar over the park flapping their legs like wings instead of driving through like normal people.

"Corey, I want you to go to the rock over there and wait for me."

The kid whined in protest, but R.J. fixed him with a steady gaze, silently enforcing the request. With another soft whine, Corey slinked away. His dejected stance made R.J.'s gut churn. Damn, he felt like a bully. He'd done the same things to countless other kids without a qualm. This time seemed different.

R.J. turned away, taking Corey's acquiescence for granted. Corey would ultimately decide whether to follow his orders or disobey him. A sudden vision of Corey submitting to him in bed took him by surprise. He stilled, his pulse hammering in three distinct and loud beats. He fought his body's natural reaction even as fast-moving pictures flickered through his mind's eye. Naked bodies. White sheets. He drew a sharp breath, the vision so real he could practically smell the pungent scent of arousal. *Hell, get a grip and set an example for these kids. Mind back on the job.*

R.J. willed his erection into submission and started issuing directions. "I want you to split into two groups—one of two and another of three. While you pack

56

up your lunch trash, I'm going to give Corey instructions. I'll be back in five minutes."

R.J. strode toward Corey, his heart twisting when he noticed the younger wolf's cowering posture. He crouched beside him, stroking Corey's shoulder and scratching behind his ears. When Corey's tremors eased, he started talking. "If you fool the rest of the kids and they can't find you, I'll get permission from Hal to take you for a drink one night. I should manage to swing a drink since you're legal age."

Corey straightened, the dejected stance falling away. His pink tongue darted out, lashing R.J. over the face in a wet swipe.

Startled, R.J. laughed and Corey repeated the action. This time the damp caress took on a distinctly sexual air, and they both recognized it. Without warning the air simmered with tension, and once again R.J. contained his reaction with difficulty. Damn, he wanted this kid. His desire wasn't right or proper but, hell, try telling that to his unruly body. Even his wolf was in on the action, twisting under his skin in a demand for freedom.

"To make this contest fair, you can't leave the meadow, but there are plenty of hiding places. Use the methods of scent disguise I've suggested and you have a fighting chance. Okay?"

Corey threw himself at R.J., knocking him off his feet and onto his butt. He licked R.J.'s face with enthusiasm, crawling over him. R.J. growled in the back of his throat, and after one final lick, Corey backed off, his demeanor uncertain and cautious. R.J.'s protective urges came to the fore. He wanted Corey's natural smart-ass manner to come through, his confidence to grow. Who was he trying to kid?

Corey spoke to something inside him.

"Don't worry. You'll do great. Besides, there's a drink on the line." He followed up with an encouraging smile, and finally Corey trotted away.

He was too damn easy. That was the problem. Shaking his head, he climbed to his feet and made his way back to the other kids. "Close your eyes and poke your fingers in your ears to mute your hearing. No cheating."

Laughing and joking, the kids complied and R.J. glanced over in the direction he'd seen Corey last. He couldn't locate him now. He waited for a few more minutes before touching each of the kids on the arm to signal they could open their eyes again. With the time up, he offered further instructions.

"I want you to track Corey. Remember every sign or clue you uncover to help you to locate him. I've told him not to leave this meadow. You'll find him hiding somewhere in this clearing, and you're to stay in this vicinity too. You have five minutes. Everyone clear?"

With a hand signal, he sent the kids scuttling off in pursuit of Corey. R.J. checked his watch and leaned against a spruce trunk while he watched. A couple of them actually paused to scent the air. The other group charged around the clearing, making so much noise every animal in the vicinity departed. They'd learn. That's what made this job satisfying for him. The kids arrived knowing scarcely a thing about their heritage and they left with a sense of pride and confidence.

He scanned the meadow for signs of Corey, grinning when he still couldn't locate him. The meadow wasn't large. The kids would find Corey before the five minutes ended.

Five minutes passed without a jubilant cry and, surprised, R.J. pushed away from the tree. "Okay. Corey wins," he shouted. "Everyone over here."

"I can't believe we didn't find him," Maria said, sashaying toward R.J.

The kids, apart from Corey, gathered around him.

"Corey!" R.J. hollered. He paused, and when Corey didn't emerge, he whipped his T-shirt over his head. "Wait here while I find Corey. If anyone moves from this spot, I'll put them on kitchen duty for the next week. Clear? Is that clear?" He waited until they nodded, before stripping the rest of his clothes, rapidly shifting to wolf.

At the back of his mind, he heard the kids comment on his shift and start wondering about the process. He already had a good grasp of Corey's scent since he'd stroked him in wolf form. Following his nose, he ran along the scent trail left by Corey. When he came to the stream, he jumped over. When he couldn't find the trail again, he splashed into the water and followed the stream, searching for paw prints. The kid had done a good job following his suggestions to fool the kids. The trail ended at the base of a tree. He glanced up and found a naked Corey shuddering in a fork of the branches.

R.J. growled and backed up, waiting for Corey to come down. When Corey didn't move, he enforced the suggestion, louder this time.

"Is that you, R.J.?" Corey's voice quavered, his brown eyes big in his pale face. The change had messed up the kid's black hair. Now it was a mixture of chestnut and brown with odd black streaks. He appeared noticeably younger with his natural color shining through.

R.J. considered shifting to human form again but didn't want to stand in front of Corey without his armor of clothes. The kid behaved bad enough now without additional encouragement. On the other hand, with the way he looked right now, perhaps he wouldn't react to R.J.'s nakedness. He went to the tree trunk, gazed up at Corey and yipped several times before stepping back to wait.

Slowly, Corey climbed down the tree. R.J. tried not to stare at Corey's bare ass. God, he'd never experienced trouble keeping his thoughts off sex before, not like this. The kid was too young. Their backgrounds were too different. R.J. didn't have any family now while Corey came from a rich and powerful one.

With Corey safely down, R.J. turned and trotted back to the rest of his charges. His tail lashed back and forth. When he realized he was displaying the distinct sign of agitation, he stilled the movement. R.J. didn't need the kid to realize he was getting to him.

"Will the shift always hurt like that?"

Relief rippled through R.J. The kid sounded steady, his behavior and stance far better than the earlier shivering. Corey would be okay, but R.J. wished he knew why he'd shifted when the residue of suppression drugs should have halted the change. Maybe Hal would have some idea.

When they reached the other kids, R.J. shifted and rapidly pulled on his clothes. He sat to pull on his footwear, studying Corey surreptitiously to make sure he was dealing okay. Good. He seemed none the worse for his experience.

"Damn," Corey said without warning, a fierce frown distorting his face.

R.J. and the other kids whirled to look at him.

"What are you so bent out of shape for?" John asked.

"You're lucky," Teague said. "You shouldn't have any problems shifting again."

"Yeah," Scott said. "You shifted. We can't yet."

"You will soon—a few days at most." R.J. turned his attention back to Corey. "Problem?"

"Yes." Corey held out his hand and shook his fingers in front of R.J.'s face. "Look at my nail polish. It's ruined."

CHAPTER FOUR

THE FOLLOWING WEEK...

"I can't believe you promised the kid a drink," Hal grumbled, although a twinkle lurked in the depths of his eyes.

"An incentive. You didn't see him. The kid was scared stiff. The change shouldn't have started early like that, even if he missed his pill. Did you take another look at his medical records?"

"Yeah, there wasn't anything unusual in the file. I've checked everything available. We could contact the L.A. pack, but I'm reluctant to cause ripples. The last thing we need is for officials to poke their noses into our business. A whiff of something out of the ordinary and they'll investigate."

R.J. nodded, understanding Hal's hesitation. Both of them avoided contact with officials whenever possible. "I hoped you'd find something I missed. It's probably best to keep an eye on him. We don't want Enforcers to arrive out of the blue."

Hal paled. "Hell no! Those guys are butchers."

He and Hal met for the first time after Enforcers killed R.J's family for refusing to take the suppression drugs. Hal had placed R.J. with a trusted friend and, when R.J. was older, he'd offered him a job. He'd worked for Hal ever since.

"One drink, I promise," R.J. said. "A beer won't be a problem."

"As long as the other kids don't find out," Hal said in a dry voice.

"I can swing one outing and the other kids will never know of our drink."

"And if he blabs? What then?" Hal picked up his pen and tapped it three times on the desktop. "Although he seems to favor his own company."

"And his art. It's the age gap," R.J. said. "The few years between them make a difference at this age. I don't think he'll tell the others."

"Okay, but if this backfires, you're on your own." Hal met his gaze before glancing down at the papers on his desk and tapping his pen again.

"Thanks. A single beer. That's all. Nothing will go wrong." R.J. understood Hal's position, especially since Hal reported to the board that financed the program. Some werewolves didn't approve of getting back to nature, despite the arguments in favor, and only allowed the program to continue because of the revenue generated.

Hal laughed. "Get out of here before I change my mind."

R.J. left Hal's office with a spring in his step, a sense of anticipation lightening his mood. Oh, his mind was clear—a drink was a bad idea. Interacting with Corey in an adult situation sent an erroneous message, but he intended to go ahead and take Corey for a drink anyway.

Wrong. Wrong. *Wrong!*

Yep, he told himself this a dozen times, heck, a hundred times. But he'd promised Corey, and he didn't go back on his word.

He made his way to the dining room where most of the kids congregated at this time of the day. "Anyone seen Corey?"

One of the girls waved a hand. "He went off with his sketch pad. Said he wanted to draw a tree." Her wrinkled nose told R.J. her opinion of Corey's spare time activities.

"Thanks." R.J. retraced his steps and put his wolf senses

to good use. Starting from the cabin Corey shared, he gradually separated the scent trails, latching onto Corey.

Instead of going in the direction he presumed Corey would take, the trail headed along the road and up a hill. Fifteen minutes later, he found Corey halfway up the hill, bent over his sketch book in total concentration.

"You're gonna miss dinner if you dally much longer." R.J. noted the fine tremor of surprise that jolted Corey. He hadn't heard his approach because he'd been engrossed in his artwork.

"I didn't hear you coming."

"That's obvious. You need to stay aware of your surroundings. It's not safe to zone out."

"I live in the city," Corey said with a return of his former attitude. "Nothing is going to happen to me there, not in the places I hang out at least."

R.J.'s brows rose and he bit back a grin. Corey didn't pull off the smart-ass attitude as well without his heavy black makeup. To Corey's frustration, every time he shifted to wolf, his makeup and hair color distorted with the change. Sometimes, his wolf form bore smudges of black. The other kids teased Corey and he'd given up trying to wear his cosmetics.

Now R.J. found him hard to resist, which made his search for Corey sheer lunacy.

"I owe you a drink," he said. "Would you like to go tonight?"

Corey's eyes widened. "You mean it? I didn't think you'd actually take me for a drink."

"I promised."

"Aren't you worried I might make a move on you?"

R.J. met Corey's laughing gaze without a flinch. "Yes."

"But you're still taking me?"

"Yes."

Chuckling, Corey closed his sketch book and stood. "Let's go. You know I'm going to do my best to seduce you?"

"There's no future to a relationship between us. You'll go back to the city."

"A future?" Corey's brows squeezed together before a grin smoothed out his forehead. "It'd be a holiday fling."

"A short-term affair?" Ever since the first day, R.J. tried not to think about Corey in a personal light. He'd fought to keep a professional mien, but Corey's words ended his internal battle. Suddenly new possibilities—ones he shouldn't consider—entered his mind.

"At the end of the summer I'll return home to Los Angeles while you'll stay here."

"This isn't a proper topic of conversation." R.J. cursed inwardly. Damn, he sounded like an uptight school mistress. "Are you coming or not?"

"A drink sounds like a fine idea." He gestured at his black jeans and T-shirt. "Should I get changed?"

"We're not going on a date," R.J. snapped and strode away.

Corey grinned, grabbed the rest of his drawing materials and sauntered after R.J. Suddenly his evening held great promise. R.J. was acting defensively—a good omen. Earlier today, he'd caught R.J. studying him in a clandestine manner. And the day he'd unexpectedly changed to wolf, R.J. had calmed his panic with both his touch and his composed demeanor. R.J. hadn't treated him like an idiot. He hadn't shouted or threatened bodily harm like his father would have under the same circumstances. Instead, he'd taken Corey's change in his stride and given Corey a task to help him focus on something else.

During the last couple of days Corey witnessed the same deft manner with the other kids during their first change. The depth of caring brought a warm, happy sensation to Corey. He lengthened his strides to catch up with R.J.

"Where are we going?"

"We'll drive down to Old Faithful."

"Will we have time to explore? Can I get my camera?"

"Sure. Meet me in the staff parking area in five minutes."

"Are we taking the bus?"

R.J. snorted. "No we're not taking the bus. Five minutes."

Corey watched him stalk away, his attention drifting to R.J.'s ass. As much as he loved his art, the desire to become physically closer to R.J. took the majority of his attention these days. He'd started dreaming about him—X-rated dreams full of sweaty, raunchy sex.

Aware R.J. waited for him, Corey broke into a lope, snatched up his camera and wallet and hurried to the parking lot.

He found R.J. waiting by a gleaming black SUV.

"Get in." R.J. climbed behind the wheel and started the engine before Corey even opened the door to jump into the vehicle.

"Man, what's climbed up your butt." Corey slammed the door and clicked his seat belt into place.

"My better judgment," R.J. growled.

Instantly, Corey decided to stop teasing R.J. in case he changed his mind and they stayed at camp. "I can't wait to visit the thermal region. I've heard it's impressive and different from the rest of the park."

R.J. shot him a curious glance. "Your family is

well-off—they have to be to afford to send you here. Didn't you go on school camps or for family vacations?"

"This is the first time I've been out of L.A." The lack of travel hadn't bothered him before, but now he hungered to see more. His father wanted him to join the firm of architects he headed. Corey forced the untenable thought away. This was one argument he intended to win. His father might have forced Corey to attend this camp, but he'd find his son less tractable on his return. He intended to pursue his art—one way or another. Corey relaxed in the passenger seat, studying his surroundings with more interest than he'd shown during the journey from the airport into Yellowstone.

The road climbed, winding around the side of a mountain. Large pines and fir trees clung to slopes and filled the flatter land. Brief glimpses of green meadows brought the urge to run and explore in wolf form. Pink, white, yellow and orange wild flowers dotted the meadows. Corey had no idea of their names and made a mental note to do some research. Hand-painted flowers always proved popular on souvenir greeting cards.

"The views are incredible." An understatement. Once they reached the highest point of the road, Yellowstone spread out before them in a visual feast. "Can we stop?"

"Maybe another time."

"Okay." Corey inhaled and R.J.'s scent filled his lungs. Immediately, the passing scenery didn't enthrall him as much. The past few days had strengthened his resolve. His stomach tightened and his hands balled to fists in his lap. He wanted R.J., and tonight he intended to make his move. He didn't think R.J. was indifferent to him. Corey wasn't even nervous. An attraction shimmered between them, growing bigger and more substantial with each passing day. All he needed to do was prove to R.J. he was adult enough to handle a covert affair for the length of his stay in Yellowstone.

Corey asked questions to while away the drive to Old Faithful township. They startled several pronghorns grazing near the edge of the road and passed more bison.

On the approach to Norris, Corey detected the faint scent of sulfur. His nose started to tickle seconds before a sneeze exploded from him.

"Sometimes the sulfur is stronger than others," R.J. said, smirking at him.

"Where are we going to have our drink?"

R.J. shot him a quick glance before turning his attention back on the road. "I thought we'd go to one of the lodges or inns, but if you want to take some photos, we might stop at the store, grab a couple of beers and maybe some snacks since we're missing dinner. How does that sound?"

A private picnic for two. An excellent idea, but R.J. didn't appear too sure about his suggestion. "That sounds like a plan," Corey said, badly wanting to spend time alone with R.J.

R.J. grunted and kept driving. Hiding a smile, Corey studied the scenery they passed. The waters of a small lake glinted between the trees, the last rays of the sun suffusing the view with light and shadows.

The edgy silence continued until they entered the small village. R.J. parked in the gigantic parking area, now mostly empty since the day visitors had departed for home. He shut off the engine.

"You coming?"

"I didn't know if I was invited to go into the shop with you."

"Don't be an idiot." R.J. strode away, leaving Corey grinning after him.

Corey jogged to catch up and fell into step with him. "Are you always this grumpy? It's no wonder you don't have a boyfriend."

"I have sex."

"You don't need to sound defensive about your love life." It was fun teasing R.J. because he bit so well. "Can we get some potato chips? And maybe some sandwiches?"

Half an hour later, they pulled up at a picnic spot near

a thermal area. R.J. grabbed the cold beers along with the bag of snacks they'd purchased.

Corey picked up his camera and followed, pausing to take photos of a boiling mud hole. R.J. backtracked to wait patiently at his side. Corey half expected a complaint or a brusque order to hurry. His father would have certainly objected to his dawdling. He decided to push his luck a little more.

"I need some perspective in my photo. Can you stand by the railings?"

R.J. did as he bid without argument.

"Thanks for bringing me here." Corey snapped another two photos in quick succession. When R.J. didn't answer, he turned to gaze in another direction and took more photos of steaming, chalky white cliffs. A cover for his unease. Nerves simmered low in his belly, his awareness of the other man acute. He wanted to touch R.J., but his normal confidence teetered now they were truly alone.

What if R.J. didn't want him and this...yearning was a figment of his imagination? He sighed, his hands trembling violently when he pushed the shutter button of his digital camera. Damn. He scowled at the result in the small digital screen. Maybe the blurry shoot would inspire an Impressionist painting.

Corey hesitated, pondering his next action. He needed

to do something because he might not have another opportunity like this with no one in sight apart from R.J.

A kiss.

He wanted to at least kiss R.J. and taste him, and give himself a tactile experience to fantasize about when he was alone. Lord, not even his first kiss with another man had thrown him to this extent. He trailed R.J. along the path until they reached an open spot with space to sit in safety.

"You want a beer now?"

Yes! An opportunity to sit beside R.J., to get closer. Corey swallowed, attempting to settle his nerves and answer with a degree of sophistication.

"Sure." Before he could make himself crazy worrying over how to make his move, he dropped to the ground beside R.J. Their shoulders brushed and the worst of his unease settled. He wanted this. Without letting himself overthink the situation, he turned to R.J. and leaned in to kiss him. Their noses collided briefly before Corey adjusted the fit and their lips settled together.

R.J. tensed and, for an awful second, Corey worried he'd shove him away. To counteract, he gripped R.J.'s shoulders, curling his fingers into R.J.'s flesh, willing to fight a rejection. His fears didn't materialize. Instead, R.J. let out a harsh groan and lifted his head. They stared at each other and a shudder worked through Corey.

R.J.'s gray eyes darkened, doubt swirling clearly in their depths. "This is a mistake."

Yet he didn't move away, which gave Corey hope. "It's not a mistake. We're attracted to each other. I keep telling you I'm not a kid. Why can't we spend time together while I'm here?"

"I...nobody knows I'm gay."

"Nobody knows I'm gay either. I can exercise discretion. I won't tell anyone or behave in an inappropriate manner in front of the others. I'd never embarrass you." Corey's heart thumped while he waited for a reply. Disappointment would strike hard if R.J. rejected him.

"This isn't a good idea."

"I'm an adult, R.J.," he repeated, trying to reinforce the point. "I'm not suggesting a forever relationship. Why can't we have some fun together? We wouldn't hurt anyone." Back home in the city he never lacked for a sexual partner. This urgent desire to persuade R.J. to agree to a closer relationship was new, a bit confusing and scary. "What do you think?" His diffidence would have made his friends laugh if they'd witnessed it. "R.J.?"

"Aw, fuck this," R.J. said. "I'm tired of fighting."

He leaned in, closing the distance between them, and grasped Corey's shoulders. Gently, he pushed until Corey sprawled back on the ground. Then he kissed him—a full-out, toe-curling mating of lips. Corey groaned at the mix of sensations boiling through his veins. His arms wrapped around R.J.'s neck, clinging in case he changed his mind.

His fears soon faded.

R.J. dominated him with his larger frame, taking control of the kiss and leading the way. His tongue demanded entrance, and Corey's lips parted, silently encouraging R.J. to take more. While he'd enjoyed sex and making out before, this was miles better. The palpable connection between them, the way the kiss throbbed through him all the way to his toes. Besides, he genuinely liked the older man and respected him.

R.J. deepened the kiss, tangling their tongues together, shooting arousal through Corey's sex-starved body. A hungry moan escaped him when R.J. slid his mouth across his jaw and down his neck. The slight suction sent happy messages skipping to his cock.

Good. Sinfully good.

His hips canted upward, bucking against R.J. in a silent demand for more. His mind raced ahead. They needed privacy. Plenty of time so they could wallow in the experience. A vision of R.J. bending him over the back of a sturdy chair, spreading him wide, flickered through his mind. Sensations flooded him, adding layers to his pleasure. The cool wash of lube over his hole. The masculine scent of musk. He groaned as blood crowded his cock. Desperate for friction and greater intimacy, he jerked his hips upward.

"R.J." His breathing came hard and choppy, damp sweat sticking his clothes to him. Unbidden, his imagination continued with the vision he'd conjured. The slippery brush of fingers, the initial intrusion and the piercing slide of a digit into his body. Heat sparked in him, his balls drawing tight until he desperately strained for control. He gripped R.J.'s shoulders, afraid to let go because of the storm buffeting both his mind and body.

R.J. slid his hand under his T-shirt and plucked at one of Corey's nipples. The small jolt of pain rippled the length of his body. Like a tsunami, he couldn't fight the building pleasure. His hips jolted, the swollen tip of his cock digging into R.J.'s hip. He gasped, shocked at his swift journey toward orgasm, yet unable to do anything except ride the wave to conclusion. The spasms went on and on while R.J. held his shuddering body, whispering reassuring bits of nothing in his ear.

Finally Corey stilled, his muscles relaxing as wetness from his release seeped into his jeans.

"Oh God," he finally muttered, heat filling his cheeks. "I'm embarrassed. I didn't mean to lose control." Corey closed his eyes, mortified by his lack of restraint. The sudden easing of weight on his upper body panicked him. "Don't—"

"Don't what?" R.J. brushed a kiss over Corey's lips.

Corey swallowed, an audible sound of anxiety. He searched R.J.'s face for a clue as to his thoughts. "Leave. Don't leave me." Hell, R.J. had the whole poker face working for him, and Corey couldn't read shit.

"Don't worry. I'm not going anywhere. I thought we'd take a drink now. How about a beer?"

"Ah, yeah. Okay." Corey sat up, grimacing at the damp spot in his jeans.

R.J. handed him an open bottle before getting one for himself. They sat together in silence, watching the steam drift off the cliffs surrounding the mud pools, the musical bubble of the mud helping to fill the silence.

For once, Corey didn't have a smart-ass comment. He didn't have a clue.

"You sure you can keep things quiet?"

Corey's breath caught at the implication. Joy burst inside him. R.J. was considering a vacation fling. "I give you my word. I won't tell anyone."

R.J. nodded. "For the record, this isn't a good idea, but I'm bloody tired of fighting you."

"Yes!" A victory. Corey fisted his free hand and pumped

it in the air.

"You're a menace, kid. You've only been in Yellowstone a few days and you've created an upheaval." His lips twitched a fraction, as if he were holding back a chuckle.

"You say that like it's a bad thing."

"You have no idea." R.J. took another slug of his beer and offered a sandwich to Corey before taking one himself.

Corey grinned and ate his sandwich with gusto. Everything in his world was right—not even the uncomfortable wet spot on his jeans dampened his sunny mood.

"I can't take you to my room."

Corey understood R.J.'s need for privacy even though a flash of hurt shot through him. "So we can meet outside somewhere. It's summer. The weather's good. Can we go somewhere tonight?"

"Not tonight."

R.J.'s abrupt reply wasn't what Corey wanted to hear. He reminded himself R.J. had kissed him and agreed to take things further between them. R.J. would keep his word. Although he wanted to object, part of him sensed a test, one he was determined to ace. He would take his cues from R.J. "Okay. Do I have more time to take photos?"

"We can stop at some of the other view points on the way back to camp."

"A couple more photos." Corey finished his beer and shot to his feet. He grimaced at his jeans, bearing the distinctive wet spot. Anyone with half a brain would guess what he'd been doing—part of the tale, at least.

"I have a spare pair of sweatpants in my SUV. I'll get them for you while you take your photos."

Corey hesitated before nodding. "Thanks."

R.J. watched Corey bound away and start snapping photos. He rubbed his hands over his face before he collected the trash from their picnic and carried the remnants back to his SUV. What the fuck was he doing with Corey? Setting himself up for a fall, that's what. But when Corey kissed him every shred of good sense flew from his head. He'd wanted to feel again, savor the physical contact of the kiss.

Corey was so open in his responses. Honest. R.J. grinned suddenly. Quick, too, which reminded him about the sweatpants. He grabbed them from the back and set the pants on the passenger seat. He'd probably turn his nose up at them because they were blue instead of his signature black.

He watched the kid take photos of a lone pine tree covered with white powder from countless different angles before trotting back to him like a frisky puppy. Corey made him feel immeasurably older. Maybe he should reconsider. Too many things could go wrong, yet the need to touch Corey ate at him. Now he'd tasted Corey and heard the hungry sounds of passion he made when he came, and there was no backing away from the knowledge. The sounds would haunt him in the coming days and drive him to seek out the kid.

"You ready to go?"

"Sure." Corey took one final shot.

"The sweatpants are on the seat." R.J. watched Corey from the driver's seat, through the open passenger door.

"Thanks." Corey's zipper sounded loud in the silence of the wilderness, the faint rustle of clothing seductive. R.J. couldn't have torn his gaze away if he tried, not for this, his own personal strip show. Corey slid both jeans and boxer-briefs—black of course—down his legs, stepping out of them with natural grace.

Damn, he was cute. Although he was still young, his body held the promise of the muscles he'd grow into, given his werewolf heritage. Corey grimaced at the blue pants and R.J. bit back a smirk.

"Don't you ever go outside? I've never seen anyone so pale."

Corey jerked upright, his eyes widening. He held the

sweatpants in front of his groin.

"You weren't shy before."

"I...I sort of feel at a disadvantage here." Corey stared at him with his big brown eyes and gnawed on his bottom lip.

"Pursuing a sexual relationship is your idea. If you want to change your mind you'd better let me know."

"No. No, of course not. I want this between us." And holding R.J.'s gaze, he lowered the sweatpants. His cock stood out from his groin now, and R.J. studied the steely length, hungry for the closer intimacy to come between them.

Swallowing, R.J. turned away to stare out the windshield. Not now but soon.

They stopped at several view points on the way back to Tower-Roosevelt camp. When they were almost back, R.J. pulled into the Tower Fall parking area.

"Wait," he said when Corey would have leapt from the SUV. "We need to talk before we get back to camp. Maybe this isn't such a good idea."

Temper snapped in Corey's face. "No, we've already agreed. I want this, and I've promised I won't do anything to jeopardize your position here."

"We won't have much time together." Damn, Corey was young. Despite giving his word, what would happen if rumors started flying? He marshaled his thoughts, about to tell Corey they needed to maintain their student-teacher relationship and leave their connection at that.

"My parents sent me here because they consider me a rebel and they thought a change of scenery would help me see things their way. I want to pursue my art. My parents don't consider art a manly pursuit, which is another reason why they sent me here. I didn't have any choice. Please treat me like an adult and let me own my decisions. I have a temper at times, and in the past I've indulged myself, letting loose with tantrums. I haven't done that here. Please, R.J., don't treat me like a child."

R.J. listened to Corey's impassioned words, understanding and sympathy making him nod. He understood Corey's frustration. During his time in the city he'd been like a trout out of water with the numerous rules and regulations. The minute he'd arrived at the park his uneasiness faded and he'd started to feel comfortable in his skin. A sense of belonging was important to a wolf. Normally pack fulfilled this need. Yellowstone and his students plugged the hole for him.

"All right. We'll do this one day at a time. If things become too difficult we stop."

Corey opened his mouth as if he wanted to argue, and R.J. wondered why he'd agreed to an affair. Corey's father ran the L.A. pack and had links to the government. Rumors circulated about the Enforcers taking out wolves who caused problems for the top hierarchy. It wasn't only the weres who refused to follow procedure and take drugs that died.

Corey nodded. "Sounds fair. I agree."

"Okay. Go and take your photos of the falls." He watched Corey amble away, his gaze wandering Corey's body, finally focusing on his tight ass. His breath eased out and a cynical laugh escaped, the chuckle mocking in the confines of his vehicle. This situation was a bloody formula for debacle, yet he ached to sink his cock into Corey and savor the physical closeness. Yep, potential for a real cluster fuck, but he intended to go ahead anyway because Corey stirred a yearning in him. Corey made him think of possibilities and the future.

CHAPTER FIVE

NAKED BODIES DIDN'T FAZE R.J. Male or female. Nudity came with his job of training the students, but Corey challenged his willpower. R.J.'s balls ached. His cock stuck out like a damn flag on a pole. And worse yet, Corey recognized R.J.'s control teetered like a child's seesaw. Up and down. The damn kid twitched his naked ass in R.J.'s direction at every opportunity.

"Today I'm going to demonstrate how to track prey." Hopefully, he'd manage to concentrate enough to teach the kids something. "I want you to follow me. Keep close, study the tracks and the signs I use to follow prey. I intend to quiz you once we get back to human form."

"What happens if tourists see us?" Beth frowned at the strands of her long hair she held in her left hand before lifting her gaze.

R.J. sometimes worried about Beth. Patiently he repeated the instructions he'd given them a few days ago. "Behave like any wild animal. Keep away from them."

Teague cocked his head, eyes brimming with laughter. "What about wild wolves?"

Maybe he hadn't hidden his impatience as well as he'd thought. "Same goes. Don't approach them. If they try to engage, retreat and find me." He enjoyed an uneasy truce with the wolves, and if they registered the kids were under his protection, they'd keep their distance. "Any other questions?"

"Will you kill something?" Maria wrinkled her nose, apprehension clouding her face. The sentiment echoed on several of the kids' faces.

"Depends. Many wolf hunts end in failure and the wolf goes hungry. The same is true of us. We'll play this hunt by ear. The object of the lesson is to apply the theory we've learned since you've been here at camp. Change now and we'll move out."

R.J. watched his six charges shift, approval filling him when he noticed they'd quickly become used to the pain and disorientation of the transformation. This part of his job, he enjoyed—watching the young werewolves mature in their behavior and attitude. The wilderness changed everyone. It was a pity only the kids with rich families and a few scholarship recipients managed the opportunity to learn about their werewolf natures. Some of the administrators and pack leaders would benefit from a run on the wild side.

The rules hurt werewolves and took the fun and spice out of life.

"Usual rules apply. Pick a buddy, and watch out for each other. If you get cut off from the rest of us for any reason, we'll meet back here."

His eyes narrowed when one of the guys paired up with Beth. Although male and female pairs were practical, these two weren't suitable buddies. "Not you two," he said sharply, fixing them with a steely glare. "John, you go with Maria. Teague, you're with Corey."

R.J. ignored the whines and growls of disapproval to step back and shift. The change surged through him, his bones cracking when they reshaped, flesh rearranging over his altered skeleton. For an instant, his eyes blurred and everything wavered in front of him, then his sight sharpened and his surroundings stood out in blinding clarity. R.J. lifted his head and howled, letting his joy ring through the hills. Corey trotted up to his side and seized the opportunity to rub against him. He nuzzled R.J.'s face before joining his song with his own higher-pitched howl.

The rest of the kids picked up the call and soon wolf song echoed through the small valley. He laughed inside. Not much chance of a successful hunt considering the racket. They'd scare every sensible animal in the vicinity with their joyful chorus.

Corey nudged him again and licked across R.J.'s muzzle. The contact sent a lash of inappropriate arousal rushing through his body. He growled, a demand for Corey to back off. To his relief, the younger wolf obeyed, but the glint of teasing intelligence in Corey's wolf eyes suggested he'd crossed the boundary on purpose. Not that he'd take the kid to task for his cheekiness. Touch came as part of the wolf nature and cemented the pack together.

With arousal still roaring through his veins, he set off at a brisk trot. Despite his pace, he still scented the air and carefully scanned his surroundings.

Somehow, he needed to arrange a private meeting with Corey. It was either that or endure another lonely solo performance, which did nothing to quell the raging need writhing through his veins.

Tonight.

Corey always jaunted off in his spare time, his sketch pad or his camera in hand. No one would suspect anything if he vanished after dinner.

A plan.

R.J. dragged his mind back to the present, trying his best to focus on teaching the kids about tracking and stalking prey. He continued his steady pace, pausing intermittently to test the wind and study the trail ahead.

Behind him, a branch cracked with the force of a gunshot. R.J. winced. Despite his lecture on moving silently through the undergrowth and his demonstrations during the past two days, the kids stomped like a herd of bison in a tizzy. He halted and turned to face them, a low rumble vibrating his throat. A warning to take care. They froze, and R.J. wanted to laugh out loud at the tableau they made. He let out another growl, this one slightly reproving. Only Corey was brave enough to give a submissive whine, and that, too, made him want to chuckle. He eyed them for an instant longer, silently enforcing his will before continuing. This time they attempted to glide rather than crash. In truth, they weren't too bad. By the end of the three months, they'd shadow a trail like pros.

R.J. caught a whiff of an animal. Pronghorn or maybe a mule deer. He slowed, searching for signs to tell him how long ago the animal had passed along the track. A broken twig, still partially attached to the bush. Some fresh droppings. Not too long ago. He slowed even more, his exact footfalls indicating to his students to take extreme care.

Glancing over his shoulder, he grinned. They practically quivered with eagerness, even the girls who remained squeamish about the idea of making a kill.

Satisfied with their progress, R.J. turned back to the trail, stalking quietly past the overhanging bushes. The trail opened out and he froze.

Three mule deer grazing in a sunny clearing.

Anticipation brought a quiver. He ghosted closer, using the terrain to his benefit. He slinked along the ground, choosing his foot placement carefully. Two deer continued to graze. The third jerked up his head. Damn. He sensed their presence.

R.J. collected himself, ready to spring. Before he could strike, two of his group broke rank. They sprinted at the animals. One deer gave a shrill alarm, and the three animals burst from the clearing.

Sighing inwardly, R.J. sat on his haunches to watch. Corey joined him, edging closer when R.J. didn't protest. When he didn't recall the kids, the others joined in the manic chase. Only Corey stayed behind.

Once alone, he rubbed against R.J. He whined, backed away then pounced at him in a playful manner. Corey's tail wagged. A low rumble came from his throat. He butted heads with R.J., backed up and pressed his weight down on his forequarters, his raised butt wriggling to encourage R.J. to play.

What a change a few days made. The rest of the group wouldn't go far. Confident enough in their abilities not to get lost, he turned to Corey and allowed his emotions to slip free. With a sharp yip, he sprang. They rolled together, over and over, snapping and mock-growling at each other. Carefree fun, yet a sort of foreplay. He grabbed Corey's scruff, pinning him and growling at the same time. Corey froze, trembling violently, a whimper of arousal squeezing past his teeth. R.J.'s cock started to lengthen, the soft, needy sounds coming from Corey driving him. God, he wanted Corey. Right now.

But not in wolf form—not for the first time.

Gritting his teeth, he let his imagination free. First he'd stroke Corey all over, explore his body and touch him in every inappropriate way possible. Finger his hole until he stretched. Suck his cock and taste the first heady drops of pre-come. Lick his balls and feel them draw tight as Corey gave in to the seduction.

Hell, yeah. He wanted to feed his cock into Corey and take him in hot, easy gliding strokes until he exploded. R.J.'s head fell back, tension ramping up inside him. He fought for control.

They'd revisit this another time. Soon.

But for the first time he wanted human form and easy communication. Regretfully, R.J. backed away. When Corey gave a soft, broken whine, he darted close to lick him. He rubbed against Corey in a sensual manner, dragging in his scent and soothing both Corey and his own impatience. A sense of happiness filled him, and he licked Corey's face, letting a yip of joy escape.

With a final lick, R.J. backed away. Aware of the passing time he called his students, his summoning howl ringing out loud and clear. A bird sitting in a nearby tree took off with an indignant squawk. Corey wandered into the grassy clearing and, while they waited for the others, R.J. watched him stalk a mouse. At the last instant he let the gray creature vanish into the tall grasses.

Pride burst inside R.J. The kid could have made a kill. He remembered everything R.J. had taught him. What more could a teacher want?

Soon the kids trotted into the clearing, tongues lolling out after their exuberant chase.

One of the course objectives was to promote fitness. R.J. thought ahead to the coming night. Yeah, he'd tire them out with a run and finish up the session by going through the correct procedure when tracking an animal. An evil thought coalesced in his mind. Maybe he would give them a quiz. Make his earlier threat into truth.

When the last panting student ran up to him, R.J. headed out, setting a steady pace. He hoped Corey managed okay, not that it mattered. He was happy to take control tonight.

R.J. finally located Corey after a half an hour search. He'd required every one of his wolf senses to track the kid down. He found him sitting on a large rock at the top of a hill, his hands moving rapidly across the page as he sketched a grizzly bear feeding on carrion.

"At least you have the good sense to do your sketch from a distance," R.J. said, dropping onto the ground beside him. He shrugged out of his day pack and placed it on the ground beside him.

"I do listen to the lectures you and Hal give us."

"I've noticed, but you didn't the first day."

"You changed my attitude. I decided nonparticipation would hurt me in the long run. Pissing off my father didn't matter anymore." Corey turned the page and stared at him before he started drawing again. "I can't believe you made us run so far today."

"You weren't too tired to hike up here with your sketch book."

"To tell the truth I don't remember walking up here. I zone out when I'm planning to sketch."

"You missed dinner again."

"I asked Hal if I could grab something from the kitchen. He told me to go ahead."

R.J. nodded, pleased with the changes in Corey. "I brought food with me."

"I don't need a nursemaid." A sharp note entered Corey's voice. "I'm capable of looking after myself."

"Of course you don't." R.J. bit back a rueful smile. He remembered saying the same thing to Hal when he was around Corey's age. Stubbornly, he'd gone his own way. Despite what Corey thought now, he probably didn't want isolation, to be ostracized and expelled from his pack. If it wasn't for this job, R.J. would have little contact with other wolves. The lack of wolfish companionship would drive him crazy. Wolves needed contact with others of their species to survive. The law and security of a pack. Something he'd lost and only found again when Hal offered him this job. Shoving aside painful thoughts of his past, R.J. sent a lazy grin in Corey's direction.

Corey's pencil raced across the page, a slash of lines, shading. He glanced at the bear before he put pencil to paper again.

"I packed lube."

The pencil slipped and spoiled Corey's perfect line.

R.J. laughed, unable to help himself.

"What?"

R.J.'s lips quivered. "Lube."

Corey scowled at him. "What about it?"

"I brought some with me."

Interest bloomed in Corey. "Yeah?"

"Yeah."

Corey slapped his sketch book closed and scrambled to his feet. A faint trace of color crept into his cheeks. "Where?"

"Follow me." When he'd first arrived at Yellowstone, he'd explored the area around the camp, knowing he'd have times when he needed respite from the kids. He'd come across a private clearing and a small stream. The spot spoke to his need to get back to nature and he intended to share his discovery with Corey.

"Where are we going?"

"To one of my favorite spots." A sense of eagerness filled R.J. along with something less tangible. Rightness? Well-being? He wasn't sure. The elusive sensation was foreign to him. Uncomfortable.

"How do you expect me to walk with a hard-on?"

"Patience, grasshopper." A smile tugged at his lips, an astounding reality for him. *Temporary*. This was a temporary fling. The months would pass rapidly and Corey would return to the city. They came from opposing worlds, were at different stages in their lives. A permanent relationship was impossible, no matter how much he wished otherwise. "A ten-minute walk. That's all."

Corey groaned, but R.J. noted his careful movements and conscientious foot placement. His stern lectures had sunk into at least one of his students.

"You're moving well, despite the erection. I can scarcely hear you."

"Thanks." Corey sounded pleased.

R.J. continued down the faint trail at a brisk walk. The kid wasn't kidding about the difficulties of walking with a hard-on. Ever since he'd made the decision to take this relationship a step further, he'd become a walking erection. *Patience, grasshopper.* This wasn't something to rush, not if they wanted to keep their sexual relationship secret. Their private meetings required careful planning.

"Are we nearly there?"

"A few more minutes," R.J. said, the impatient note in Corey's voice stroking his ego. He continued up the narrow track, climbing effortlessly. Behind him, Corey started to breathe more heavily, and R.J. slowed a fraction. The last thing he wanted was an exhausted lover. Oh no. He had big plans for the younger wolf.

Finally they arrived in the tiny clearing. Apart from the lack of frequent visitors, the spot held the advantage of position. They'd hear anyone approaching long before they arrived.

R.J. let his pack slide off his shoulders. He opened it to pull out a blanket. With a flick of his wrists, he spread it on a patch of springy grass.

"We're going to have sex in the open?"

"We're going to fuck on this blanket." Tension ramped up inside R.J as he voiced the words. During the small hours of the morning he'd dreamed of this, jerked off to the residual heat generated by those dreams. Now he finally had Corey in a private spot, he couldn't wait to make his fantasy into a concrete reality. He bent to remove his footwear and rapidly stripped his clothes, tossing them carelessly aside.

His smile in Corey's direction probably appeared predatory. Ravenous hunger for Corey's body certainly filled him. His gaze skimmed Corey's black T-shirt and jeans, the desire to finally glide his fingers across his pale skin bringing an uncharacteristic tremor to his hands. He curled them to fists, wincing at the bite of his claws into his palms. His wolf stirred uneasily, pushing for command of his body and startling R.J. in the process. A loss of control. That's what Corey did to him.

"Take off your clothes. Now." His barked order jerked Corey into action. He flung his clothes off with abandon, his chest rising and falling along with his rapid breaths. His gaze didn't leave R.J. the entire time.

For the first time, he allowed himself to examine Corey solely with the eye of a lover instead of teacher, studying the pale skin revealed as the kid stripped. After days spent in the sun, his skin no longer bore extreme city paleness. Soon the constant exercise would burn away the last of the baby fat covering his muscles. Not that Corey seemed like a kid, especially with his erect cock jutting out like a tracker dog scenting prey. R.J. let his gaze follow the lines of Corey's body.

"If all you're gonna do is stare, I'll get my sketch pad out again. Put your nakedness to good use."

R.J. lifted his hands in the universal sign to stop. "Stay right there. I haven't let myself study you before. Too dangerous."

"I've looked at you."

"I know." R.J. remembered the strength of will he'd required to control the reaction of his unruly body whenever he'd felt the weight of Corey's stare. "You have to behave when we're in public. No one can discover we're fucking each other."

"What? I'm your guilty secret?" A trace of hurt colored Corey's words.

"I warned you. Remember? You agreed. You knew the deal going in." R.J. almost caved and apologized for his snappish tone, but there was too much at stake for both of them. He hardened his heart and went with his fears. "I don't want to lose my job." His job meant everything to him, his salvation after the loss of his family. For a long time he'd dreamed of revenge, searching for the man he'd seen commit murder from his hidey hole. It was Hal who convinced him to let the past go. He'd drifted aimlessly until he returned to Yellowstone to work with Hal. "I don't want to cause problems for you with your family either."

Corey frowned. "Would you lose your job if they discovered your sexual orientation?"

"Maybe. Maybe not. I will lose my job if someone finds out I'm having sex with one of my students. Your father will want my head."

"Maybe we shouldn't do this then."

"Do you want to return to camp?"

"No!" An adult mien settled on Corey's face. "I'll be more careful. I promise."

R.J. pushed aside his foreboding. He'd battled with himself about this move ever since he'd first seen Corey and couldn't fight the attraction any longer. "I can't decide where I want to touch you first."

Corey grinned. "I can offer a few suggestions."

R.J. dropped onto the blanket and patted the empty

space beside him. "Come here."

Corey voiced a hoarse curse and pounced, landing on top of R.J. Their bodies slid together while they playfully rolled and wrestled each other. Then they shifted position and settled, fitting together like matched puzzle pieces, their cocks grinding together in sync. Groaning, Corey spat out another coarse oath.

"Easy, kid." R.J. transferred his weight. They still embraced but not as intimately. "Let me touch you, taste you." Slowly, he lowered his head and brushed his lips over Corey's. Corey moaned and curled his hands around R.J.'s neck, plastering their bodies together again.

It was easy to see Corey wanted hard and fast. He writhed, mashing his body against R.J., his breath emerging in harsh pants of need. Although every part of him screamed to hurry, to go along with Corey's silent suggestion, R.J. purposely took his time, savoring the fire and chills warring within his body.

He dragged in a breath, caught a shot of pine from the surrounding trees and the musky scent of pre-come. Corey's hand ran from his shoulder, down his side and came to rest on his ass. Like a shock from a livewire, the touch zapped him from his head to curling toes. Corey's caresses felt even better than he'd imagined, and the visuals...the pale smooth artist hands kneading his muscles.

Corey's hands wandered from R.J.'s sight, fingers straying to his crack. They delicately parted the globes of his ass and teased his hole.

He'd never last if he let Corey touch him intimately. Aware of the urgency thrumming between them and his own teetering control, R.J. reached behind to grasp Corey's hands. "I'm not going to last long if I let you touch me."

"One of us has to touch." Corey moved his hands a fraction, squeezing his butt cheeks. "Besides, I love to touch. It's an artist thing."

R.J. smacked at Corey's hands. "Don't disobey me. I'm in charge here." The light of laughter glowed in Corey, and R.J. half-cursed and chuckled at the same time.

"Or what? What will you do to me if I misbehave?"

"Shit, I shouldn't have set a challenge like that. I know better."

"I react well to dares."

"I know." R.J. flopped over on his back, mock-frowning at Corey's irrepressible grin. Corey's scent filled every breath he took, pushing his desire higher. A groan escaped. "I wanted to go slow. The second you touch me, all I can think about is spreading you and pumping inside your hole."

Corey inhaled sharply. "That's a bad thing?"

"I don't want to hurt you."

"You'd never hurt me. You'd cut off your front paws before you physically hurt me."

Corey's certainty rang through his words. R.J. let his gaze wander freely across Corey's naked limbs, long legs, partially erect dick. A hard shudder racked his body. "God, I want you." Along with the physical need came the foreign yearning he didn't understand.

"Then come get me." Corey rose on all fours and waggled his butt in R.J.'s direction. "I'm not gonna fight you." He grinned over his shoulder, eyes bright with sexual excitement. "I'm yours for the taking."

Total acceptance. R.J. closed his eyes, worried the emotion might boil over. No one ever accepted him this way. Not his foster parents, their pack or past lovers, and until the words rang between them, he hadn't realized he craved approval, affection. The acknowledgment was a heady sensation, and he hugged it tight, feeling the self-imposed bonds within him break. His eyes opened, the change in colors indicating he'd started the transformation to wolf. He had to swallow to focus. "Let me grab the lube."

Corey huffed out a hard breath. "At last. Some action." He waggled his bottom again, but this time R.J.

recognized the younger man's barely concealed anxiety. He held concerns. Probably not about the sex, but doing it with R.J. or the fact he might change his mind. The last of R.J.'s self-control unraveled at the knowledge.

"Come here."

"I thought you were getting the lube."

"I want to kiss and pet you." Something else unusual for him. Usually his casual encounters happened quickly with minimal contact, a mutual scratching of an itch before they parted ways. Most times he didn't ask for names or pay attention to his lovers' faces. And he seldom kissed.

He dropped a quick peck on Corey's forehead. "Lie flat on your back, close your eyes and listen. No touching," he added when Corey's hand rubbed his cock. "I'm the one who's gonna make you hard. If you're good, I'll use my mouth."

Hell, listen to him. No way on Earth did he intend to leave this spot without tasting Corey. R.J. intended to swallow him down, right to the root. A little growl emerged from him, the acute craving for Corey a hard knock to his equilibrium.

"I'm starting to think you're all talk." Corey stealthily reached down to stroke his cock, his mouth stretching into a challenging grin.

"Maybe. Maybe not." R.J. didn't bother with a warning

this time. He pounced, his weight squeezing the *oomph* from the kid's chuckle. Too impatient for finesse, he grabbed both of Corey's hands and held them above Corey's head. For an instant, he stared at his lips. When the kid's tongue darted out to lick them, R.J.'s heart thumped against his ribs in a staccato beat. Hungry. So hungry for this. Hell, he was starved for Corey. He couldn't wait a minute more.

"Leave your hands where they are, out of the way."

Dipping his head, warmth met his lips. A hint of mint. He applied pressure and Corey opened for him. Their tongues slid together and R.J. was lost. He nipped, licked and tasted, angling his mouth for the best position.

The thirst for more, for greater intimacy, sprang at him like a testy old bear. Their stubble rasped together as R.J. trailed kisses across Corey's jaw. The salty flavor did nothing to deter him, the savage throb in his groin driving him to demand more from Corey. He pressed a kiss on Corey's neck, nipped the fleshy part where shoulder and neck met. Slowly he moved down Corey's body, inhaling his scent, the heat of desire stabbing them both.

"Oh fuck." Finally Corey moved his hands from where R.J. had placed them. They burrowed into R.J.'s hair, massaging and tugging enough to make his scalp sting. "I'm not gonna last long." As if to illustrate his words, his hips jerked upward, rubbing his cock against R.J.'s hip. A wet trail of pre-come eased its way over his skin.

"I'd better hurry then." R.J. moved down and swiped his tongue down the middle of Corey's chest. Like him, Corey didn't have much in the way of chest hair. He dipped his tongue into Corey's navel, loving the tremor of awareness shaking the kid. Going lower still, he raked his tongue across Corey's abdomen.

The scent of arousal filled his every breath. His and Corey's. He ran his fingers down Corey's shaft, along the top and back up the vein on the underside. As he watched, a bead of liquid formed on the slit. R.J. licked his lips and bent over to lap the drop away. Corey whimpered and damn if he didn't want to echo the sound. With a rough growl vibrating in his chest, he took Corey into his mouth, traveling past the point of no return.

Chapter Six

Another man had never rocked Corey's world this much. Not even his need to become an artist drove him this hard. He inhaled, blowing out a harsh breath. A tremor stunned him. Heat surrounded his cock and R.J.'s tongue busily explored the swollen head, delving and retreating only to return to tease again. His entire body vibrated, singing with the pleasurable sensations. R.J. sucked him deeper, swirled his tongue with expertise. His throat swallowed around his tip, then he pulled back to lick away every fresh drop of pre-come.

"R.J." A moan escaped when R.J. started playing with his balls. Harder and harder, R.J. pushed him until pleasure coursed over his entire body, his pulse racing so fast he worried about his heart handling the pressure. Unable to stop himself from moving, his hips pumped into the air, forcing his cock down R.J.'s throat, overburdened nerves pushing him toward climax.

Corey's hand crept to his nipple. He fingered it and tugged hard. The sharp twinge of pain traveled straight to his groin. His balls pulled agonizingly tight. A hungry noise broke from his throat, the delectable torture pulling his face into a grimace. And still R.J. kept licking and sucking, his fingers working Corey's balls, driving him crazy. The hard squeeze should have hurt. Instead the raw pressure escalated his surge into pleasure.

"Oh hell. Fuck. Fuck!" This was *way* better than he'd imagined. More, somehow. He wanted to tell R.J. how much each touch blew his mind, to voice his acute satisfaction. He opened his mouth to say something more articulate. Nothing emerged except a croak.

R.J. continued to suck. One of his fingers glided past Corey's balls to push on the smooth patch of skin between there and his hole. He tapped his finger sharply, the vibration jolting Corey. Heat curled into all the small spaces in his body, the uneven beat of his heart thundering like a storm inside his mind. The sensations twisted, coalescing into a giant wave.

A sob emerged and he bucked deeper into R.J.'s hot mouth. Color flashed behind his tightly closed eyes.

The tsunami swept over him, dragging him under. His ejaculate exploded from his cock, the spasms of pleasure continuing for long, drawn-out moments. The storm in his body quieted. Gradually, their surroundings swept back to his consciousness. R.J. gentled his touch, cleaning him off with a swirl of warm, wet tongue.

Corey opened his eyes and stared at R.J. Their gazes connected and held, the atmosphere thick with sensual tension. Corey licked his lips and swallowed. "Can I take care of that big boy for you?"

R.J. snorted, his mouth twisting into a grin. "That sounds like a bad line from a porno movie."

"Got it in one," Corey said. "I get my best lines from the movies. I want you inside me. Make me feel the burn." His lines might sound corny but he meant every word. He bit his bottom lip to control the moan of pure need building at the back of his throat. When R.J. didn't move, Corey swallowed. God, surely R.J. hadn't picked this moment to harness his scruples? So far, he'd enjoyed every second. When he returned to his cabin he wanted to remember their joining and experience the tiny twinges of pain, the by-product of a good pounding. "Here. Do me now." Ready to force the issue, Corey plucked the bottle of lube off the blanket and tossed it at R.J.

R.J. caught the bottle automatically and stared at the

label.

"Come on," Corey snapped. "You're not changing your mind now. Remember, this was your idea. You want to drive me crazy?"

"Damn, that's scary. You sound like an adult."

The words cut to the quick, although Corey didn't let his pain or indignation show. If he reacted badly, he would be behaving childishly. "I am an adult. I know exactly what I'm getting myself into. I need you."

Seeming to snap from his trance, R.J. popped the top on the lube and squeezed some into the palm of his hand. "Lie on your back. My wolf's too close to the surface. I'll control myself easier if I can watch your face."

Not wanting R.J. to change his mind, Corey repositioned himself with alacrity. He spread his legs and started to stroke his cock. "Take me. Don't worry. I won't break."

"That's the one thing I'm not worried about." He slapped Corey's hands away from his dick.

"Just trying to speed things along."

"You'll learn I do things at my own pace."

Corey waggled his eyebrows. "As long as something happens today, before we turn old and gray."

R.J. scanned Corey's body, a slow visual sweep, and a shiver of awareness pelted Corey. From his face to his groin, R.J.'s gaze stroked him. Corey's cock stirred with renewed interest. A quick rebound.

"You're beautiful."

"Me?" An unexpected compliment, and not one he'd anticipated from R.J. "I drive my father crazy with my makeup and nail polish. I embarrass him. He cringes every time he sees me."

"I don't want to talk about your father."

"Neither do I." Corey gave R.J.'s cock a furtive stroke. "Isn't the lube drying out on your hand yet?"

"Stop copping a feel." R.J. slapped Corey's hand and slid his fingers across Corey's thigh. He stole a quick breath, anxiously waiting for R.J. to give him more. The first brush of R.J.'s fingers across his pucker pulled a gasp from him, despite the sun-warmed lube. The push into his hole brought a soft curse. Yeah, R.J.'s touch was way better than anything he'd dreamed of, and this was only the beginning.

"Okay?"

"More than okay." He thought R.J. might go slow and tease him again. Didn't happen. To his relief, R.J. slid his finger deep, slicking his channel with the competent stroke. Oh man. Corey lifted his hips into the smooth glide of fingers, encouraging more of the same. Felt damn good. The addition of another finger filled him, stretched him. R.J. spread his fingers in a scissor motion to widen him even more. Probing fingers caressed and stroked, and when they hit his gland for the first time, Corey jerked at the jolt of electricity surging through his body. His balls pulled tight, drawing up again in preparation. At this rate it wouldn't take long for him to spill his load again.

"More," Corey gasped. "Fuck, give me more. Please. I need you now."

When R.J. removed his fingers, his empty channel pulsed. Corey inhaled sharply, battling for control. Nerves simmered in the pit of his stomach, which told him more than anything how much he'd come to care for R.J. This was more than a mere vacation fling for him. A confession wouldn't pass his lips because the last thing he wanted was for R.J. to stop this delicious torture.

The bottle of lube burped when R.J. squeezed more on to his hand. He slicked up his cock with economical strokes, his lazy pleasure ratcheting up the lust in Corey. He couldn't wait to see R.J. at the moment of climax.

R.J. sought his gaze. "You ready?"

"Yes, damn it." Tension worked down his body and converged in his balls. He was past ready and so grateful they didn't need to use condoms. Human lovers expected condoms so he used them to avoid questions. He and R.J. didn't even discuss the matter because werewolves didn't succumb to the same human diseases.

R.J. shifted his weight and pushed inside Corey. When the head of his cock rested just inside, he paused. "I think I'm gonna like this."

Corey squirmed, desperate for deeper penetration. "I never pegged you for such a damn tease."

A surprised expression slid across R.J.'s face. "I...hell." He buttoned his lips and thrust hard.

The intrusion burned. Corey bit his lip, enjoying every twinge as his channel expanded to fit R.J. Corey couldn't decide whether to close his eyes and concentrate on the sensations or to leave them open and watch R.J. Either way he couldn't lose.

"God, you feel good. Tight. Fuckin' perfect." R.J. pulled back and invaded again.

Mesmerized by the sight of his lover, he gawped at R.J. His gray eyes were squeezed tight, his face a contorted mask of pleasure.

"Kiss me," Corey pleaded, suddenly needing R.J.'s hard emotion focused solely on him. A rich rush of desire made his pulse skitter, pushing him quickly to a place of raw need. His hips canted upward, forcing R.J. to plunge deeper. "Faster. R.J., please go faster."

"My pace." R.J.'s eyes snapped open, and Corey witnessed the wildness in them, the flicker of wolf. R.J.'s fingers dug brutally into his hips. He'd have bruises come tomorrow. Corey didn't care.

"More," he whispered.

R.J. withdrew, slid back inside until he was balls deep. He paused to lay a bruising kiss on him. Their lips clashed, Corey's hands clutched R.J.'s shoulders, clinging to him like a tree to the earth. Pulling back a fraction, R.J. thrust in earnest. Hard and aggressive strokes that made Corey's eyes roll back. He snatched a breath. Their mouths fused, and he moaned into R.J. when a wild stroke slid over his prostate. Oh man. Fuck, that was good. Corey drifted, lost in the sensations, the heat, the pleasure.

R.J. sank into the hilt, groaned and gave in to the hunger evident on his face, orgasm twisting his features while his cock pulsated. A flood of wetness filled Corey. Corey reached between them to get himself off again, but R.J. slapped his hand away. With the perfect amount of pressure, he gripped Corey's cock and squeezed. Corey's belly muscles tensed, his balls swelled and he came.

Fuck. The pleasure swept him again like a wild storm. When he returned to himself, he slumped, relaxed and replete.

R.J. touched him and he acted like a wimpy marshmallow. Yep, when it came to this man, he was plain easy pickings.

"You okay?"

"Hell yeah." Corey brushed aside the twinges of discomfort in his body. "I'm more than okay. When can we do that again?"

A slow, sexy smile lit R.J.'s face as he pulled free. "That good, huh?"

"Yes." For once Corey kept his cockiness at bay. He hoped R.J. realized how sincere he was with his words. This situation between them was no longer a challenge or a game for him. The days would pass rapidly, and there'd be times when he and R.J. couldn't find privacy. He let out a sigh. Now that he'd been with R.J., he didn't want to think about the end.

"It felt good on my end too. Better than good." R.J. stood. "Fancy a run before we return to camp?"

"Hell yeah." Corey leaped to his feet and started his shift before R.J. changed his mind. He'd come a long way when it came to embracing his wolf, never hesitating. This struck him as kind of ironic. R.J. had to hunt most of them down whenever it was time to change back to human form. Maria and Beth whined about ruined fingernails, but not him. Well, only that one time. Some of them couldn't wait to get back to the city and their luxurious amenities. He'd give his left nut to spend more time in Yellowstone, especially with R.J. in the equation.

A few days later R.J. strode into the dining room for breakfast. His gaze zoomed straight to Corey, and he couldn't hold back his grin when he received a cheeky wink in return. Unable to help himself, he joined Corey and Teague. "Are these seats free?"

"Take a pew." Teague jerked his head at one of the two spare chairs.

"Coffee?" Corey asked.

A warm sensation flared to life in R.J.'s chest. "You don't have to wait on me."

Corey leaned closer, his eyes twinkling with mischief. "I'm trying to get the inside scoop on our activities today. I thought a cup of coffee might work."

"Good idea." Teague eyed the blackboard menu. "I'll put in our orders. Pancakes all round?"

"Works for me," Corey said.

"Thank you," R.J. said. "Pancakes sound great." He waited until Teague wandered out of hearing. "Are you okay?"

"Couldn't be better. I have a very sexy lover and the afternoon off. Could we do something? Together?"

"I'm sorry. It's my turn to be on call." Regret chased through R.J. because he'd like to have more one-on-one time with Corey. "I thought if you and the rest of the kids were interested, I could take the bus down to Old Faithful. We can return to camp via Yellowstone Lake."

Although disappointment flickered across Corey's face initially, his eyes lit up at the idea of some sightseeing. "I'd love to take more photos."

A slow smile bloomed in R.J. He'd suggested the afternoon trip to Hal already, hoping the kids would enjoy the outing. Actually, Corey had given him the idea and now, seeing Corey's pleasure warmed him through.

"Teague, R.J. is taking the bus out this afternoon to Old Faithful. We'll get to do some sightseeing," Corey said when his friend returned.

"Awesome," Teague exclaimed. "Since we're not allowed our phones, I want to get a disposable camera. They've run out at the shop here. What are we doing this morning after breakfast?"

"More tracking exercises. We're having a contest against Hal's students."

"Is there a prize?" Corey asked, a gleam of challenge in his eyes.

Understanding came to R.J. immediately. Corey would like to score more private time with R.J. along with a beer. "I might buy ice creams for everyone at Yellowstone Lake."

"Make that chocolate and it's a deal," Corey said. "For chocolate I'd do my very best tracking."

Later that afternoon, R.J. parked the bus outside the Old Faithful service center. "We'll spend an hour and a half here. Everyone meet back at the bus at two-thirty, and we'll head off to Yellowstone Lake."

"Will we see Old Faithful?" Beth asked.

"We have fifteen minutes before the geyser erupts. I know some of you want to purchase cameras. I'll show you where the store is, and I'd suggest the rest of you find a vantage point and save a place for us all to watch the eruption. Any questions? No? Okay, let's go."

The kids dispersed rapidly, leaving R.J. alone with Corey. R.J. allowed himself the luxury of touching Corey's biceps. "Go and save me a good spot, okay?"

Corey flashed him a quick smile and sprinted away, leaving R.J. to lock up the bus and hurry to the store. In the store R.J. helped the kids find what they needed and sent them on their way before making his own purchases. He left the store with his own disposable camera, so he could take some photos of Corey and the rest of the kids, and half a dozen chocolate bars.

Aware of passing time, R.J. hastened his pace and arrived at the geyser as water and steam burst from the vent. Sulfur filled every breath, and he started to breathe through his mouth in an attempt to stave off a sneeze.

"Man, this is cool," Corey said, his finger pressing

feverishly on the shutter button of his camera.

"How high does it go?" Maria asked, bouncing up and down in excitement.

"Up to 180 feet," R.J. said.

"The brochure says it keeps going for five minutes," Teague said.

"I can't wait to paint it," Corey said.

R.J. took one look at Corey's shining eyes and thrilled at the shared experience. He rested his hand on Corey's shoulder and squeezed gently. It didn't matter that they weren't alone or they weren't having sex. He wouldn't have changed this moment for anything.

"Today we're going to practice tracking," R.J. said.

"More tracking?" Beth squawked. "You've had us practicing for the last three weeks."

Teague nodded. "Yeah, that's all we've done since our trip to Old Faithful. When will we do something new?"

"Tracking and using sense of smell play a big part in the lives of wolves. We use smell to find food, to sense danger and to recognize family," R.J. countered.

"I like tracking," Corey said.

"Suck up," Teague said.

"And you're good at it." Beth wrinkled her nose when everyone sniggered. "The tracking, I mean. That's why you like it."

"If everyone is done with breakfast, we'll head out," R.J. said. "Don't forget water and your lunches.

An hour later, R.J. parked the bus at the trailhead. Hal set off with his students, and R.J. collected his group together. "We're going to do our tracking in the valley that lies to the west of here. We'll walk along the rim to the far end of the valley and start our tracking exercises—with Hal's group today. Follow the path just ahead." He lifted his hand to forestall questions. "Hal and I will fill you in on the details before you shift. Off you go."

R.J. took the rear, and Corey dropped back to walk at his side.

"I'm sorry we haven't had a chance to meet in private," R.J. said in an undertone. "I don't want you to think—"

"I know you're busy and have responsibilities," Corey said quietly.

"I enjoy spending time with you, even with the group." R.J. swallowed, hardly believing the words he'd uttered—even if they were completely true. "I've never said that to anyone before."

Corey slung a companionable arm around his shoulders and grinned. "I'm glad you picked me. Are you going to give me some hints about our tracking exercise?"

"Nope," R.J. said cheerfully.

An hour later they reached a vantage point. With views over the valley below, the spot was ideal because the surrounding trees and undergrowth provided privacy. On the valley floor below, a herd of bison grazed. Perfect for their exercise.

"Gather round," Hal said. "The twelve of you will work together today. I want you to decide on one animal, cut it from the herd and harry them as if you're intending to snack on them for dinner."

R.J. scanned the eager faces in front of them. "You'll need to sneak up on the herd and get as close as you can without detection. Choose your animal and take turns at forcing them to run."

"That sounds like hard work," Maria said, her tone close to complaining.

Hal shared a rueful glance with R.J. "Most wolf hunts end in failure," he said. "And the pack goes hungry. Use this as a learning exercise to apply the skills we've taught you."

"Listen to Hal," R.J. said. "This is an opportunity to practice for the hunt at the end of the course. Remember to choose an animal that appears weaker in some way. Maybe they're younger and vulnerable, less experienced or perhaps injured. That will make your job easier."

"You'll find this painless if you work as a team. Keep

your competitiveness out of this exercise and it will go well," Hal said. "R.J. and I will observe from up here. Send up a distress howl if you need us."

An acute sense of anticipation filled the air as the kids stripped and shifted. Corey trotted over to him in wolf form and nuzzled his legs. Grinning, R.J. stooped to scratch the scruff of his neck. "Have fun."

With a low yip, Corey trotted off to catch up with the others.

"Corey is a natural leader," Hal said. "He's surprised me. I appreciate the way you've taken an interest in his training. He's blooming with your attention."

"I've been impressed with Teague too," R.J. said gruffly. "The rest of my group tends to look to them for leadership. Do you want a drink?"

"Sure, it's going to take a while for them to get down into the valley basin."

They spent the passing minutes in companionable chat.

"I see them," Hal said.

"That's not good," R.J. said, craning his neck for a better view. Each bison had lifted its head, no longer focused on grazing. "The herd has noticed them too."

"Hell, I don't believe it. One of the kids is after that calf. They should know better than that. The mother won't like them getting close."

R.J. shook his head, not taking his gaze off the kids and bison below. "Sometimes all the telling in the world won't make a difference. They need to learn from experience. You taught me that."

"Look there's the mother."

"And she's about to charge."

"This is the stage where I always wonder if I should be down with them," Hal said, frowning. "Damn it, back up. Give the mother some space."

R.J. didn't take his attention off the unfolding drama. "You say that every course. We have to let go some time."

"Who is that?" Hal asked.

R.J. narrowed his eyes. "Damn, it looks like one of my girls. Maria or Beth. They should know better."

As they watched, another wolf distracted the mother, leaping at her nose. *Corey.* The mother whirled and lashed out with a hind foot. The bison cow lowered her head and charged. Corey dodged. The cow whipped around and charged again with barely a pause. This time she caught him a glancing blow. Corey lay on the ground, stunned.

R.J. cursed, fear making him clumsy as he ripped off his boots.

"It's all right," Hal said. "He's moving. The other kids have things covered."

R.J. let his knees complete their buckle and dropped his

butt to the ground. His heart pumped rapidly, taking time to slow to its normal rate. "Some of my teaching must've stuck." Damn, he couldn't seem to stop shaking.

"You like the kid," Hal said.

R.J. focused on Corey, his wolf twisting, shoving against his control. "Yeah. Now that he's dropped his smart-ass attitude he's intelligent and fun to spend time with. I like him a lot. Do you want me to go down and check on him?"

"They haven't signaled us. Besides, he doesn't appear badly injured."

"Thank God." R.J. watched the young weres regroup and start again with Corey directing the show. "We owe him a couple of chocolate bars."

"At the very least," Hal agreed. He took his gaze off the kids to turn to R.J. "You make a fine teacher. I'm proud of you, R.J."

A lump formed in R.J.'s throat, the praise rare. Treasured. He swallowed once, and again, to shift the emotion in him. "Thanks. It's easy with students like Corey."

THE MONTHS PASSED RAPIDLY, the summer days filled with lectures, running and hunting in wolf form, working on his art and spending stolen moments with R.J. A shudder of pure desire worked through him when he recalled the fiery lovin' the previous night.

Corey picked up a stack of dirty plates from breakfast, pleased with the mindless task because the chore allowed him to wallow in his memories. He stacked them into the dishwasher and recalled the clandestine meeting.

"Face the wall and put your hands above your head on the wood." The hoarse demand greeted his arrival behind the empty cabins at the far end of the camp. The danger of discovery sent a frisson of desire spearing to his cock. Slowly, he followed R.J.'s instructions, his pulse beating erratically. Although unsure of R.J.'s agenda, he liked this surprise side—the dominant lover who expected him to obey an order. He liked the fact R.J. wanted him enough to risk exposure.

R.J. nuzzled his neck, breathing in his scent. His tongue stroked the shell of Corey's ear, bringing a shiver. While the sensations coursed through his body and the moist lap of R.J.'s tongue distracted him, hands reached around to unfasten his belt. The rasp of his jeans zipper sounded overly loud, and Corey cringed, almost expecting someone to investigate the noise. He bit his lip, attempting to contain the moan of excitement struggling to break free.

Competent hands pushed his jeans down his legs

and slid inside his boxer-briefs. R.J. grasped his cock, smoothing his thumb over the crest.

"You want me."

"Always." The undeniable truth. R.J.'s presence and especially his touch turned him on in an instant.

"This is gonna be quick." R.J. pressed a knee between his legs, silently encouraging him to spread them farther apart. "Can you keep the noise down?"

"Yes." Anything to persuade R.J. to continue with his stroking and caresses. "I can keep quiet."

An abrupt rustle indicated R.J. rearranging his clothing. A cool finger stroked his pucker. A jolt punched through his body. No matter how often R.J. touched him, each time brought something new and memorable, an experience to savor when he returned to the city.

Corey scowled at the wall. It was something he didn't want to think about. Shifting his focus back to his lover, he waggled his butt in a silent demand to get a move on.

R.J. chuckled. "I've never met a more impatient kid in all my life."

"I'm not a kid."

"Figure of speech. I wouldn't be here if you were a kid." He cupped one ass cheek, stroking then smacking without warning.

"Ow!"

"Shush." R.J. massaged his entrance, and Corey bit back a groan, startled by the cool lube. Also impatient, he was relieved when the push of R.J.'s cock stretched his hole. He widened his stance and pushed back against the intrusion.

"Easy." R.J.'s hot breath brushed his ear. They slid together, silent as they took their pleasure. Some people might say furtive but Corey found their loving perfect. Hot. R.J. thrust hard. One hand grasped Corey's cock while the other clutched his shoulder. Higher and higher they soared until R.J. grunted and the hot rush of come filled him. R.J. pressed against his back, squashing him against the cabin wall. Corey didn't care. With the hard wood against his cheek and R.J. at his back, he came with a heated rush of pleasure.

In silence, they righted their clothes. This was the part Corey hated—the parting. Just once he'd like to fall asleep pressed against R.J. and spend the night in his arms. He'd like to wake the same way and have lazy morning sex before they went about their day. Sadly, a dream. In a few weeks he and the rest of the group would fly back to Los Angeles.

"I'd better go. I told Teague I intended to sketch some night scenes." Corey turned away to pick up his drawing materials.

"Wait." R.J. grasped his shoulder and spun Corey back to face him. "I bought something for you."

Corey started to say something but R.J. yanked him close and kissed him while pushing something into his rear jeans pocket. The words slid from Corey's mind and he curled his hands around R.J.'s neck. His mouth opened and he savored his lover's taste, the solid weight of their bodies pressed together. No doubt about it. Returning to Los Angeles wasn't something he looked forward to, and that day was fast approaching.

"You'd better get back to your cabin."

"You could walk back with me." Pleasure suffused Corey when he realized R.J. had given him a chocolate bar.

"If I escort you back, I'll have to punish you for leaving your cabin during the middle of the night."

A chuckle escaped Corey. "Kitchen duty?"

"Or worse."

"Teague warned me about probable consequences. He's still pissed about Hal making him peel potatoes all week."

"That's what you get for breaking the rules."

Corey winked at him. "We've been breaking the rules."

Obvious guilt had filled R.J. then. Corey recalled it and glowered at a dirty pot. R.J. didn't like sneaking around or keeping things from Hal. He said he owed Hal and there would be trouble if anyone discovered he and Corey were fucking each other like rabbits.

CHAPTER SEVEN

R.J. TRIED TO ACT normal, but his heart refused to cooperate. The final week of the summer course. Each snatched meeting with Corey was one to treasure. He stared out the window of the dining room then turned to check the wall clock. Almost time for the last run with the kids.

"Something wrong?" Hal's voice came from behind him.

Steeling himself, he turned to face his boss. "The end of a course is always a bit sad."

"Yeah, I know what you mean. It's hard not to get attached to the kids. Even Corey Wilson turned out all right, despite my worst fears."

"He's the most promising student we've had through

here for a long time." R.J. fought to keep his expression suitably composed. The last thing he needed was for Hal to become suspicious.

"I agree. Corey's a talented artist too. He was telling me his father expects him to join his firm of architects once the summer is over."

"Huh, he doesn't seem like the architect type. I can't imagine him wearing a suit."

The edges of Hal's mouth kicked up into a grin. "I wonder if he'll go back to his black hair and makeup."

"Not our problem." R.J. shoved aside the traitorous thoughts urging him to make Corey his challenge. No. No, he'd considered this in the small hours of the morning. Their backgrounds created a predicament for one. Corey came from wealth and his family held expectations for his future. They wouldn't include a werewolf with his own family history—objectors who refused to take the suppression drugs and died for their cause.

"Thank goodness he's not our headache." Hal glanced at the clock. "Time to go. I'll round up the troops."

"I've loaded the meals on the bus."

"Great. See you out front."

"In five." R.J. strode into their small office on automatic pilot. He stared at the pile of admission files ready for their short week-long courses without interest. Corey filled his mind. Only a few days until the students departed and already his heartstrings twanged at the parting.

"There is no possible future," he muttered in an attempt to set his mind straight. Cursing under his breath, he grabbed his binoculars and stomped out to the bus.

"I'll drive today," Hal said, already heading for the driver's seat. "You give them the gritty details during the journey to the trailhead."

R.J. laughed, as Hal meant him to, although to his ear, the chuckle came off forced. He'd counted on driving, having something to concentrate on instead of Corey. Every time he caught a glimpse of the kid—at present sitting with his best friend, Teague—his pulse raced. They were picking on Maria and Beth, teasing the two girls. A wave of jealousy swelled inside him. Stupid, he knew, but he couldn't help the weakness in him.

Swallowing, he picked up Hal's clipboard. Once the kids settled and Hal was underway, he started.

"Today we're aiming to make a kill. You have the knowledge necessary to bring down a deer. We've taught you the skills to track."

"I don't want to kill a Bambi," Maria said, screwing up her nose.

Teague reached over the seat and squeezed her hand in comfort. She fluttered her lashes at him like sleepy kitten.

Young love. Maria's parents would have kittens if they knew she was cuddling up to a scholarship student in her spare time.

And was he any better?

R.J. continued. "You can make your kills singly or in teams. Your kill can be small if you're hunting alone. If you're part of a team, we expect a bigger kill. Any questions?"

"How do we prove we've killed something?" Teague asked.

"If it's small you can bring your prey back to the spot where Hal and I set up camp. If you bring down larger prey, signal me with a howl and I'll come to you."

Corey cocked a dark brow, his eyes alive with excitement. "What if we fail?"

"We expect each of you to submit a verbal report to us once we get back to camp. After Hal and I hear your report you'll receive a pass or a fail."

Beth flipped her hair over her shoulder. "What happens if we have a problem?"

"Or we injure ourselves?" Maria asked. "What if our prey attacks us?"

"The attack of the killer bunny," one of the boys droned with voice-over dramatics.

"Hal and I have a fully stocked hamper with food

supplies. We have a first aid kit and a plan for every other contingency. Howl, and one of us will come running. Or, if you're working in a team, one of you come back and get us. Any more questions?" The final hunt was a time of joy and celebration of everything they'd learned.

Normally.

This time he felt as flat as a tire pierced by a sharp nail.

Hal pulled up at the trailhead. The kids piled off the bus.

"Did everyone get their water bottles?" R.J. asked.

"Yes," the kids chorused with varying degrees of sassiness because either he or Hal voiced the same question every time.

"Good. Everyone gear up for the hike to our base. We have a lot of supplies and I'm not carting them all," Hal said.

Finally they organized the kids and set off with Hal at the front and R.J. bringing up the rear. The kids were talkative today. Excitement tinged their words and manner. Most of them wore a cloak of confidence.

"Do you really fail students?" Teague asked.

"If necessary," R.J. said. "We've only failed one student since I've worked here."

"I want to frame my certificate and give it to my grandmother," Teague said. "She used to tell us stories of the old days before we took suppression drugs. She was excited when I won the scholarship here.”

“You’re lucky. My family never talks about pre-suppression times,” Corey said. “My father is too busy shouting at me.” He grinned. “I’m a trial to them.”

“You should visit some time. My grandmother likes visitors.”

“I’d like that,” Corey said.

The two young werewolves started chatting about their lives in the city, and R.J. followed in silence. Self-belief shone in both young faces. They were the two best students and would pass this final test with flying colors.

At their chosen site, the kids prepared.

“Remember, you have three hours. Hal and I will call in chorus when time is up. This is the signal for you to return. And don’t forget to keep away from bears and other wolves. Give them a wide berth.” After answering last minute questions, they finally raced off singly and in groups. R.J. watched Teague and Corey dash off together before he settled back to wait with Hal.

“Something wrong?” Hal asked.

R.J. let his frown slide off his face. “Nah, I’m a bit tired. I didn’t sleep well last night.”

“That makes two of us,” Hal said.

Surely Hal hadn’t seen him and Corey last night? “Problem?”

"Some of the officious busybodies are attempting to shut the program down again," Hal said. "Nothing I can't handle. It happens periodically. We have a hundred percent safety record. Not one of the kids has gone berserk or drawn human interest to us. They've started taking the suppression drugs once their wilderness experience ends with no one any the wiser."

"And? Is there something else?"

"Yeah. You've heard about the militant movement who reject the suppression drugs?"

R.J. shrugged. "Rumors. I presumed the talk was idle gossip and speculation."

"No. There's an underground movement, much like the old railway system for slaves. Sympathizers help move rebel werewolves across the border into Canada. From there most of them fly or ship out to Australia or Africa."

Something in Hal's stance brought R.J. to attention. This wasn't mere idle conversation. "What's going on?"

"I have a werewolf arriving later tonight."

R.J. stared at Hal, thoughts flashing through his head so fast he didn't know which to voice first. "Is this the first one?"

"No, there have been others."

R.J.'s gaze narrowed. "Your cousins from New Orleans? And the ones from Washington D.C.?"

"I didn't think I could pass off more cousins."

"You're taking a big risk."

"I know, but I can't sit back and do nothing. The suppression drugs are wrong on so many levels. There's no good reason for werewolves to live like this. The only reason we do it is to keep a few of the high-level pack members in their positions of power."

"Last I heard, voicing things like that will get the Enforcers on your tail."

"It's the truth." Hal dragged a harried hand through his hair.

"But participating is dangerous, for all of us."

Hal started to pace back and forth. "You're right. I shouldn't involve you in my cause. Forget I said anything."

R.J. grabbed Hal's arm as he strode past. "I didn't mean that. Of course I'll help you. I owe you everything. You helped me after the Enforcers killed my family. And you helped me get this job. I know there were objectors because of my history. I'll never forget everything you've done for me."

"This isn't about payback, R.J. You're like a son to me."

Warmth filled his chest. "I care for you too."

"Damn! I didn't tell you...this isn't about emotional blackmail."

"Of course not." Hal had given him so much over the

years. Shelter. Companionship. Trust. And love. He'd do anything to help Hal in return. "This is about friendship and loyalty. It's about doing the right thing. I don't agree with the suppression pills. We're lucky we're able to live such unfettered lives. I'll do anything I can to help."

"It could be dangerous."

"So? You need help. Tell me what you want me to do."

Hal gripped R.J.'s hand. "Thank you. As long as you're sure."

"Positive." Laughing, R.J. swept Hal into a hug, clasping him hard for an instant and releasing him before Hal became too uncomfortable with the contact. "You can count on me."

COREY RACED THROUGH THE undergrowth with Teague at his side. The fresh green of the ferns and bushes filled his lungs and burst through his mind until he wanted to howl with the pleasure of the experience. Not even the knowledge this sojourn would soon end dimmed his enjoyment. By common consent, they slowed their lope enough to scent the air.

Corey caught a musky scent straight away. He slowed a fraction more and Teague followed suit. Rabbit. All right!

He moved closer to Teague, giving him a swift nudge. Teague let out a soft whine of agreement and they were off, following the scent trail. This time they moved carefully, as R.J. had taught them, sliding past the plants and choosing their footing with caution. A snapping stick would alert the rabbit to their presence.

A scuttling and faint crackle of dried grasses in front of them made them freeze. Without any communication, Teague stayed in place and Corey circled to approach from the other direction. Once in position he slinked forward. *There*. The tips of the rabbit's ears moved, twitching a fraction while it nibbled on some greens.

Together they leaped, pouncing at the rabbit from opposing directions. Panicked, the rabbit jumped. It struck Corey in the chest. On instinct, he grabbed. His teeth sank into warm flesh.

The rabbit ceased struggling, dead before he knew it. He dropped the creature on the ground, hunger tearing through him without warning. No, he needed to show R.J. to prove they'd listened to every lecture. But first, they needed another kill.

They considered burying the rabbit and decided against this in case another animal stole their prey while they were off chasing their second kill.

In hunting mode again, he—carrying the

rabbit—ghosted through the forest behind Teague, pausing frequently to listen and scent the air. Teague sighted the ground squirrel first. He froze and Corey immediately followed suit.

Their second kill came laughably easy, and Corey chortled gleefully inside. Hunting was easy. They had a couple of hours to spare. Maybe he and R.J. could sneak away for a quick fuck. Despite enjoying the hunt and a part of him wanting to devour the rabbit, he'd love a juicy hamburger. As soon as he arrived back in L.A., he'd indulge the need for fast food.

The thought reminded him of R.J. and his good humor faded. Damn. He was trying to behave like an adult. Walking away from R.J. was gonna kill him.

With their prey dangling from their jaws, they trotted back toward the spot where Hal and R.J waited for them.

A whimper to the left of the path caught their attention. Corey stopped and dropped his rabbit. At his side, Teague did the same. They glanced at each other, and when the whimper repeated a second time, they approached with caution. A musky scent—familiar but not quite right—prodded Corey to vigilance.

Wolf.

Teague pressed close. Together, they inched forward over the grassy track and into the undergrowth. Rounding a corner, they came across an earth and rock scar. Small uprooted bushes withered in the relentless sun. Ripe earth and grasses rested like chunks of vomit across what was left of the narrow track. The loose dirt and rocks trembled and moved beneath their weight, shifting in a precarious manner. Alarmed, they halted, only the pained whine urging them to move again and continue across the uneven terrain.

At the far end of the slip, a rock trapped a wolf in place, snaring its front leg. Yellow eyes glared at them from a narrow face. Corey padded closer and the wolf panicked. A pained growl filled the air when the wolf strained against the weight trapping him.

Corey froze and backed away again to stand on steady ground. Coming to a quick decision, he shifted to human.

Seconds later, a naked Teague stood beside him. "What should we do? Hal and R.J. told us to avoid wolves."

"We can't leave him trapped. I can't leave without trying to help." The wolf twisted and Corey noted the swollen teats. "Her. She must have pups somewhere."

"Yeah. Okay." Teague squared his shoulders. "What's the plan?"

Corey eyed the enormous rock. "Do you think we can lift the rock between us?"

"Maybe. As long as the wolf doesn't try to fight us. Or

bite."

"If we can't shift the rock, maybe we can lever it enough to lift the wolf free." Corey scanned the area for a suitable stick to use. "You check that way. I'll go this way."

Ten minutes later they returned to the trapped wolf with a selection of stout sticks and branches.

Corey drew a sharp breath. "Let's do this."

Teague eyed the wolf. "Lady, you bite me and I'm gonna bite back."

"That sort of talk get you very far with the ladies?"

Teague grinned. "I do better than you."

If only he knew. "How should we do this?"

"I'll lever the rock and you drag her free," Teague said.

Corey studied the nervous wolf and glanced back to Teague. "Why do I get the hard part? Can't we toss for it?"

Teague gestured at his naked body. "Do I look as if I have a coin on me?"

Laughter burst from Corey. "All right. You win. On three."

They stepped closer to the trapped wolf and she growled, hackles rising to enforce the warning.

"Maybe you should flirt with her or something."

Corey chuckled. "Please, Mr. Silver Tongue. You forget I've heard you chatting up both Maria and Beth. Damn, look at her teeth. They look sharp."

"Quit stalling, Corey."

"You'd better make sure I don't bleed to death when she bites me."

"I promise." Teague ignored the wolf's growls to position the lever carefully. "Hurry, we don't have much time."

Corey started talking to the wolf in a low voice and edged closer. Those teeth looked lethal. A healthy dose of fear shot through him even though he attempted to bank his trepidation down. The wolf would catch his anxiety if he wasn't careful and that would make things ten times worse for them. Steeling himself, he kept talking and extended his hand for the wolf to sniff. All the time he moved closer.

The wolf snapped at his forearm. Teeth crunched down and pain shot the length of his arm.

"Fuck! Three, dammit, Teague. Three!"

Teague pushed down on the lever and the rock moved a fraction. Corey seized the wolf, attempting to ignore the pain where she gripped his arm. He tugged. The wolf howled and struggled. *Right with you, buddy. My arm fuckin' hurts too.*

"Teague, do something."

Teague grunted and the rock moved again.

Suddenly the wolf popped free, much like a champagne cork exploding from a bottle. Corey toppled backward and dropped her. She, thankfully, released him. Splotches of blood sprayed the ground, dripping down Corey's arm.

The wolf snarled and scuttled away. Although limping, she disappeared rapidly into the undergrowth.

"There's gratitude for you," Corey muttered.

Teague put the thick branch down. "You okay?"

"My arm is throbbing like a bitch."

"Shift to wolf. R.J. said a change to wolf form always speeds up healing. Do you think the wolf is okay?"

"What about me?" A surge of indignation zapped Corey. "I have an ouchie too."

"You'll live. We have time to track the wolf."

"How long do you think she was there?"

"Can't have been too long because she didn't seem dehydrated."

Corey shifted, wincing at the extra slice of pain that cut him when the shift took control of his body. His right arm throbbed, but the bleeding was sluggish now. Ignoring the twinge of pain when he put his weight on his front right paw, he seized his rabbit and trotted off in the direction the wolf had departed.

He and Teague followed the trail for ten minutes. At least the wolf had managed to move.

The scenery transformed from shady forest to steep and rocky terrain. They trotted from the shady forest into bright sunshine.

They saw the wolf at the same time. Three pups burst from inside a shallow cave to greet her. Their piercing cries held hunger and fear.

Without considering the matter overly much, Corey walked toward them, his rabbit dangling from his mouth. He halted a few feet away and dumped his rabbit. Giving a faint rumbling whine, Teague followed suit, dropping his ground squirrel beside Corey's rabbit. Once they'd backed up to the shelter of the trees, they paused to watch.

The female wolf limped forward and seized the rabbit. One of her pups grabbed the ground squirrel.

Without warning, a familiar howl cut through the air.

Crap! Corey and Teague shared a glance, realizing their time was up and they'd failed the final test.

CHAPTER EIGHT

THE DAY BEFORE DEPARTURE...

"I don't want to leave Yellowstone." Anguish filled Corey's voice and contorted his features until R.J. had to glance away. "Please let me stay."

R.J. swallowed, armored his heart when he'd like nothing better than to seize Corey and run off with him, preferably into a sunset. Wouldn't happen. Corey couldn't stay. Hal would ask questions, for one. Then there was Corey's father.

They had no future together. Corey would realize this too if he thought with his head.

"Your family expects you at home, and I have a job here. Responsibilities." When Corey would have spoken, R.J. continued, determined to drive a wedge between them, one to protect them both, to protect Hal and those who secretly stayed for a few days. "Don't you get it? We're too different."

"But I—"

"I'm not interested in anything permanent," R.J. broke in before Corey uttered the L word. He might suspect Corey's feelings, but hearing the kid verbalize them would totally destroy him. Other wolves would judge them. Corey's parents would judge them, reject them both. R.J. wouldn't wish an outcast status on anyone, least of all someone he loved. He steeled himself not to show a hint of uncertainty about his decision.

"So all you wanted from me was sex? A good fuck?"

"Yes." R.J. froze, not moving a muscle. He'd wanted to make love with Corey today, to say goodbye and show him the depth of his feelings. Instead this conversation was heading steadily downhill.

"Anyone would have done?"

God, he hadn't thought parting from Corey would hurt so much. He had to get away before he did something stupid.

"I have things to do before the next intake of kids arrives."

"R.J." Corey's glance implored him to change his mind. His left hand clenched, unclenched. Not. Gonna.

145

Happen.

"I'll see you tomorrow before you leave." R.J. turned his back on the man he'd come to love and admire and stalked away, hammering the wedge between them home with finality.

"Don't bother." Corey's chest ached. Anguish seared his throat, swelling it to an uncomfortable tightness. How could R.J. say their time together meant nothing?

R.J. expected him to walk away without a scene. His eyesight blurred. Angrily, he swiped the tears off his cheeks and started walking. No weakness.

He was a Wilson, dammit. Wilsons never gave up. His parents expected him home and next week he'd start working for his father. They wanted a return for the education investment.

Too bad. He intended to continue with his art.

Corey wished he could discuss his future with R.J. Something else that wouldn't happen because R.J. didn't want him.

"Corey!" Teague hollered from the other side of the camp. "We're driving down to the village with Hal. You coming?"

"Sure." Corey veered toward Teague and his other

roommates. It was probably best if he kept busy instead of stewing about R.J. He'd hoped they'd snatch at least an hour or two together today. He had to fill his time somehow.

"Are you two still sticking to your story about giving your kills to the wolf?" John asked.

"Yep," Teague said.

More teasing. Corey lifted one shoulder in an irritable shrug. "Hal believed us."

"You're full of shit," John said. "Did Scott and I tell you about the mule deer we downed?"

"In excruciating detail," Teague said dryly.

Beth winked slyly. "Come on. We've all passed the course. You can tell us the truth now. You rolled in wolf poop to make yourselves smell like a wild wolf."

"No matter what we say you don't believe us," Teague said. "We can't win."

A dead spot filled Corey and he couldn't dredge up the required laugh. He felt lifeless inside. Numb. R.J.'s rejection was like a lethal kick in the head.

A good fuck. The words pelted his mind like hailstones struck the ground during a storm. Hell. He sniffed sharply and bit his tongue, hoping the jolt of pain would help him control the seesaw emotions pummeling him. He needed a few minutes to pull himself together before he started blubbering like a fool.

"Do I have time to grab my camera? I'd like to take some group photos of everyone."

"Good idea," Beth said. "I wish I'd brought my camera. Can you email us photos when you get home?"

"Sure." Corey turned away before the others picked up on his distress. It was gonna be a long day.

EARLY THE NEXT MORNING, Corey dragged his butt from his cabin, pulling two bags behind him. Earlier he'd dyed his hair black, applied black eyeliner, mascara and lipstick. His fingernails bore a fresh coat of ebony polish. Armor in place, he silently handed his bags to R.J.

The other students were chatting together happily, exchanging email addresses and phone numbers, eager to return to their homes. Corey felt like an inmate returning to the padded cells beneath the pack headquarters.

The only bright spot was the paintings he'd managed to place on consignment with one of the Old Faithful lodges plus some of the shops. Tourists liked taking a piece of Yellowstone home with them, in this case a Corey Wilson painting.

Corey returned for his last bags. He placed them at the

rear of the bus with the others and climbed aboard. Only pride kept him to a dignified silence. He didn't intend to grovel to a man who didn't want him.

Teague dropped into the seat beside him and offered him some gum. "You okay?"

"Yeah." Corey took a piece and handed back the packet. Shit, was he that transparent? He had to work on his inscrutable face.

"Not looking forward to going home?"

Corey shook his head. "My father expects me to work for him."

"And you want to do your art. Sorry, man. That's tough." Something in Teague's tone made Corey forget about his own worries. He concentrated on his friend.

"What about you? What are you going to do?"

"I have to find a job. Help out my mom."

"What sort do you want?"

Teague worked his piece of gum. "I'm not fussy. There aren't many openings where I come from. I might have to move into the city."

"Come and stay with me," Corey said. "You can pay me board once you find a job."

"You serious?"

"Yes." It would be good to have one friend who understood the joy of running in wolf form. "Maybe someone in my pack will have a job opening. Or maybe my friend who runs the art gallery. He knows lots of people." Corey hesitated and checked to see if any of the others were eavesdropping on their conversation. "He's gay. If that bothers you, you shouldn't come and stay with me."

Teague shook his head, meeting his gaze directly. "Doesn't bother me."

Corey's breath caught as a wave of shock swamped him, rendering him momentarily speechless. Did Teague know? Corey caught his bottom lip between his teeth, the cosmetic taste of the lipstick filling his mouth. He grimaced. Nah, he didn't know anything. He would have said. "Then we'll get along fine."

"Thanks, man. I appreciate it. I'll call you once I know where I'm at."

Three Days Later...

"I'm not going to work at your firm." Corey met his father's gaze, determined to stand his ground.

"What?" His father turned away from the floor-to-ceiling windows of his office. His brown eyes glittered. Shock? Anger? Maybe a little of both. "Of course you're joining the firm."

"I don't want to be an architect."

"You have your degree." His father gathered himself, standing tall, his dark hair bristling outward like a halo. "Of course, you can't wear makeup when you join the firm."

As usual, his father only heard what he wanted to hear. Throwing his weight around worked for him—he didn't know any other way.

Corey's eyes narrowed, the only sign he allowed to escape. Tight control. Calm. He could speak with his father like an adult. This time he wouldn't cave to parental pressure. He intended to focus on his art. "No."

"What do you intend to do? Not your art?" His father sneered. "I won't have it. You'll make a laughing stock of me, your family. The pack will think I'm weak."

"Is that the only thing you care about? How you look in front of the rest of the pack?"

His father didn't deign to answer. Instead, he turned away, the matter settled in his mind. Fine. He'd make his own arrangements for the future. Corey left his father's office, entered the elevator and rode down to the ground floor.

Outside on the street, he dodged in and out of the people—locals going about their daily business of shopping and work. Tourists experiencing everything

Los Angeles offered in the way of entertainment. Three months earlier the city had felt like home, a haven, but now the buildings closed in on him, the scents of traffic and over-perfumed people plus the ever-present noise an assault on his senses. He collided with a man in a suit, busy texting on his cell phone. The combined scent of sweat, grease and aftershave made his stomach heave.

"Hey, watch it, man," the guy said.

Corey didn't bother arguing. He arrived at the bus stop, timing his appearance perfectly. The bus pulled up and he climbed aboard, longing for the fresh air of Yellowstone. The passing scenery blurred as he stared out the window. Instantly he thought of R.J., the man leaping into his mind like a wolf pouncing on its prey. The ache in his chest deepened. One thing was certain. He couldn't continue like this.

He missed R.J.

And he hated taking the suppression drugs again. He felt as if he were walking around with a plastic bag over his head, his senses dulled by the extra layer.

The one bright spot was Teague's move to the city. He'd arrive this evening. From their conversation on the phone, Teague didn't like the return to suppression drugs either, their effect on him even worse than the dampening down of awareness in Corey. Teague's wolf had faded to the point where he couldn't feel him.

God, he never wanted to get to that stage again. Hal gave them a bottle of drugs when they left Yellowstone. Weaker than the ones Corey normally swallowed each morning, the special prescription obtained by his father. Once these finished, he didn't know what he'd do. Maybe take half a pill. If WereCompliance—the group who randomly checked werewolves across the country to make sure they took the suppression drugs—tested him, the screens would show he was legal.

Treason...did he dare and could he control his wolf enough to fool everyone?

He alighted near the gallery. The more he dwelled on his departure from Yellowstone, the more he regretted walking away without arguing his point with R.J.

An adult would battle to achieve his goals. Fight for his future. Wring everything he wanted out of life.

He wanted R.J.

His wolf writhed inside him, pressing insistently against his skin. The reminder of his dual nature gave him a jolt. *Take care!*

Corey pictured the forest in his mind, painting a jungle of green over the concrete skyscrapers blocking most of the sun. He released a deep breath, imagining the warmth of the morning light, the breath of wind and R.J. prowling at his side. Instantly, he felt calmer, his wolf more settled. Straightening, he strode up the steps leading into the gallery.

Corey came to an abrupt halt two steps inside. The small wall at the far end held not a single painting. Earlier in the year, Gerald had allocated this wall to him. He'd hung several of his Yellowstone paintings the day before.

"Where are my paintings?"

Gerald lifted his head from his pile of invoices. "Oh, those. I took them down."

"Why? They were good. Some of my best work."

"The couple who came into the gallery thought the same." Gerald's smile turned into fully fledged enjoyment. "Which is why they purchased five."

Corey gaped at his boss, not certain he'd heard correctly. "They what?"

"The couple loved your paintings. I hope you have more because a man came in before and couldn't make up his mind. He returned and wanted to kick himself when he found they'd gone."

Corey sank onto a nearby stool. "I don't believe it."

Gerald rose and grabbed him in an effusive hug. "Believe it. Those paintings were great, Corey. So lifelike. I don't know what happened to you at Yellowstone, but you seem more mature. Attractive," he purred next to Corey's ear.

"Can I interest you in a night out?"

"Stop fooling around." Corey couldn't contain his grin of pleasure. He'd sold five paintings. "How much did I get for them?"

"The asking price."

"Really?"

"Congratulations, kid. You're on your way. If you can produce more paintings like that I predict a brilliant future."

"I have three more out back in the storage room."

"Make sure you hang them before you leave."

"I will!" He and Teague could have a celebratory dinner tonight. Maybe the paintings he'd placed on consignment at Yellowstone would sell quickly too.

The hours flew and he arrived back home on a real high. He clattered up the stairs to his third floor apartment instead of waiting for the rickety elevator, arriving at his door not even breathing hard.

Teague was waiting at his door, two bags sitting at his feet.

"Hey." Corey gave his friend a quick hug of greeting, the familiar scent of wolf absent. "I'm glad you're here."

"You need someone to keep you honest." Teague grinned, although his words made Corey wonder. He unlocked the door, standing aside to let Teague enter. In that instant he came to a quick decision. He might have to hide his werewolf nature but he didn't have to lie about his preference for men over women.

Not to his friend.

Of course, Teague might not react favorably to the revelation. Corey hesitated then closed the door and turned to Teague. "I'm gay."

"I figured that at Yellowstone," Teague said.

"You didn't say anything."

"It's none of my business."

Corey hadn't realized how much he craved his friend's acceptance. The relief made him feel almost giddy.

Teague's jaw dropped. "You know I like girls, right?"

Corey spluttered. "I don't think of you like that."

"Because I'm not R.J."

"You knew?"

"I slept in the bottom bunk. Every time you came in late you woke me up."

"You never said anything."

Teague smirked at him. "No, but a guy gets curious. I couldn't figure out why you always smelled like him."

"But R.J. said the pills they used to wean us off the suppression drugs made us smell alike."

"That's what confused me. It took a while for me to put the clues together."

Corey laughed, the knowledge that Teague knew the truth liberating. "I'll show you your room. It's not very big."

"I don't care. I'll start paying rent as soon as I get a job."

"No problem, dude. I sold some paintings. We're going out tonight to celebrate."

The loud ringing of the phone interrupted, the strains of a recent rap tune bringing a grimace. One of his parents. Great. Just great.

Knowing they'd call again if he didn't answer, Corey cursed and jabbed the answer button.

"Corey, I haven't seen you much since you returned from Yellowstone."

"Hi, Mom." He spoke rapidly when she paused to take a breath.

"I expect you for dinner tonight. Oops, there's the doorbell. I have to go. Seven o'clock."

"Wait, Mom. Can I bring a friend?"

"Of course, honey. Don't be late. You know what your father's like when he doesn't eat on time." The line clicked before Corey managed another word.

"My mom wants us to come to dinner. That okay?"

"You don't need to look after me."

"My father might know of someone hiring."

Teague shrugged. "If you're sure."

157

"You'd be doing me a favor. If you're at dinner my father won't have a chance to lecture me. Believe me, dinner will be more peaceful with you there."

"Don't you get on with your folks?"

"I haven't told them I'm gay for a start."

"Good luck with that. My mom always asks fifty questions. I can never keep a secret around her."

"I'm a disappointment to my father." For the first time, Corey wanted to share. "He doesn't understand why I want to draw and paint instead of design buildings."

"Do you think he'd hire me?"

"We'll find out soon enough. I might not get on with my father, but he's a fair employer. He hires a lot of pack members." Corey didn't think his father would take out his anger at his son on Teague.

An admiring whistle filled Corey's old vehicle when he pulled up at the gateway of his parents' house.

"Wow! This is where you grew up?"

Corey ignored Teague's reaction and spoke into the intercom. Seconds later the gate clicked and started to swing open.

"Just because it's big, doesn't mean we're a family." He put the car in drive and accelerated through the imposing gateway. Wow, he'd really said that. Surprise crinkled his brow and clenched his hands around the steering wheel. It was the truth. This place didn't feel like home. He'd made his own home at his apartment.

"Let's go."

"I didn't force you to bring me."

Corey turned to Teague in surprise. "What the hell are you talking about?"

"You don't seem happy about me being here." Teague gestured at the house and its obvious luxury. "I'm wearing jeans."

"You kidding?" He gestured at his own black jeans and skintight T-shirt. "Remember you're doing me a favor."

Teague scowled at him, uncertainly glimmering across his face. "You sure?"

"Positive, man. And we'll get a better dinner than anything we can scrounge at the apartment."

A maid answered the door and took their jackets—one denim and the other leather—without a flicker of distaste. Shortly after their arrival, his uncle, aunt and three female cousins appeared for dinner, too, creating yet another barrier between Corey and his father.

Feeling the weight of a stare, Corey turned his head from the conversation to meet his father's gaze. His father was a large bull of a man and one could call him handsome.

No matter how hard he searched, Corey couldn't find a bit of himself in his parent. He glanced away almost immediately, unable to meet his father's stare for longer than a few seconds. Sure boded well for their upcoming *discussion*.

Hal and R.J. hadn't made him feel worthless. Corey couldn't remember a time when his father had shown approval.

"Teague, where do you come from?" one of his cousins asked once the introduction stage finished. She fluttered her eyelashes and leaned closer.

Corey suppressed a flash of amusement with difficulty. Teague better watch out. His cousins were slobbering after his friend, treating him like male chocolate.

"How was Yellowstone?" his uncle asked.

"Fantastic," Corey said. "Teague and I met at Yellowstone."

Half an hour later, they sat around the dinner table.

"Didn't it hurt to change to a wolf?" one of his cousins asked.

Corey grimaced in memory. "It hurts like a bitch."

"Corey! Don't speak like that." His mother glared at him, her eyes narrowing in warning. Apologize or else. He'd witnessed a similar expression on his own face when his temper slipped.

Corey dipped his head in silent apology and averted his gaze. "Sorry. Yes, shifting to wolf is painful."

His uncle nodded. "So I've heard. Did you pass the course? Did you make a kill?"

Corey and Teague exchanged a grin. They'd given up trying to explain their lack of success because no one believed them.

"We ran out of time," Corey said. "They gave us a pass."

"There were humans around the day we hunted," Teague said. "Their presence made a successful hunt difficult."

"Who trained you?" His father spoke directly to him for the first time since their arrival.

"Both Hal Price-Jones and R.J. Blake conducted lessons, but mainly R.J." Corey wondered why his father wanted to know.

"Blake? Price-Jones?" his uncle questioned sharply. "Have I not heard those names mentioned at the council meetings?"

"Blake was the child who escaped the Enforcers' cull. Price-Jones petitioned for custody and later sponsored him for a job at Yellowstone."

His uncle cut a hunk of meat off his steak and shoved it into his mouth. A spot of gravy splattered on the front of his pale blue business shirt. He chewed and swallowed.

"I'm surprised he was given leave to take the job with traitors in his background."

Corey's father sipped his red wine. "We have our spies. Blake has never shown a hint of treason."

Spies? Did that mean R.J. was in danger? Hal? He shot a quick glance at Teague, saw his friend's concern.

"What?" His father noticed their exchange. "Did you notice something out of the ordinary?"

"No," Corey said slowly. The last thing he needed to do was act suspicious. "They were both great."

"Teague?" his father asked. "I'd like to hear your thoughts?"

Teague didn't hesitate. "They both acted in a professional manner." He wrinkled his nose and his lips curled into his trademark grin. "They set clear rules and guidelines. We learned a lot."

His father nodded and took another sip of wine.

His mother, bless her, changed the subject. "Are you attending the Spring dance?"

"Ooh, yes," his youngest cousin said.

The women launched into a discussion of dresses and fashion, which thankfully didn't require any input from him.

"Time for you to quit playing the field. Pick a woman and settle, boy," his uncle boomed from the far end of the table.

Corey barely suppressed his cringe of horror. He caught Teague's sympathetic gaze.

His aunt turned to his parents. "Do you have any candidates in mind for Corey?"

Corey opened his mouth and shut it again when Teague kicked him under the table. Teague was right. The last thing he needed right now was a confrontation with his father.

"We've considered about half a dozen girls," Corey's mother said.

What! News to Corey.

"You'll have to stop putting on makeup." His middle cousin let out one of her annoying girly giggles. "No girl wants her husband to wear more makeup than her."

His other two cousins joined in the giggle chorus while a pained expression marched across his father's face.

"I like makeup." Corey winced when Teague kicked him again and he shot a warning glower at his friend. His wolf stirred, sensing his irritation. A deep breath and determination tamped him down.

Corey's mother cut a cheesecake into portions and deftly served it while a maid distributed the plates. "Corey won't wear makeup during the gathering."

It was like a trap closing over him. If he didn't act soon,

he'd end up married to a sweet woman who wouldn't understand why he didn't want to spend time with her. He missed R.J., hungered for his touch. His kisses. He missed their discussions about everything—both big and small.

"Did I tell you I sold five paintings of Yellowstone at the gallery?"

"What, twenty bucks each?" His father's mouth twisted into a faint sneer, the sort that made his wolf stir again.

"Nope." A trace of smugness filled Corey. "Two thousand a piece." R.J. would be proud of him. A series of images flickered through his mind—naked limbs, two bodies. God, he missed R.J. so much, despite the way they'd parted.

"Two thousand?" A hint of respect crept into his uncle's eyes. "That's serious cash."

Corey noted the varying reactions of his family. They ranged from disbelief to doubt to avarice. His mother bore an expression of dismay. And if he wasn't mistaken, a trace of panic.

He caught his father watching and forced a smile. "Lucky I have more to hang in the gallery."

His mother bit her bottom lip before standing and picking up her empty plate. She collected several more before speaking. "We thought you'd come and live back here when you started work for your father. It would save the drive through heavy traffic every morning."

Corey aimed for matter-of-fact instead of confrontational. "I already have a job at the art gallery."

"We'll discuss this later," his father said.

"Are you dating anyone?" his aunt asked, and Corey could have kissed her for the change in subject.

Predictably, his cousins giggled. They did that a lot.

His wolf stretched in agitation and Corey breathed carefully, taking several even breaths until he calmed. "Not at present." And not in the future either.

He and Teague managed to escape about two hours later, thankfully without the promised discussion with his father.

Teague sprawled out in the passenger seat. "Your father is scary."

Corey gave a short laugh. "You don't need to worry. He approved of you. It's me who needs to worry. I still have a *discussion* in my future."

"What's wrong with working in the art gallery? My mother would be ecstatic if I earned a cool ten thousand in a day. Your parents treated your sale like it was nothing."

Corey sighed. "I don't get it either."

"What are you going to do?"

"I know what I want."

"Tell me."

"I want to spend more time with R.J."

"What does R.J. say?"

Corey pulled up at a red traffic light. "I haven't talked to him since we left. We didn't exactly part on good terms. Besides, he's not out of the closet either. I don't want to make trouble for him."

"He's not a mind reader."

Corey pressed down on the accelerator when the light changed and shot Teague a scowl. "Aren't you the Ms. Fixit today?"

"Sorry. I babysit sometimes and hear the girls talking with their friends. This crap is like rot. Sinks into the brain and festers. Once there you can't get rid of the stuff."

A snigger escaped at the aggrieved expression on Teague's face. "Aw, are you blushing?"

"Fuck off."

Corey laughed louder.

"I was only trying to help." Teague's voice sounded stiff this time, a little offended.

Corey wiped a tear from his eye and slowed to scan the road for a parking space. "I'm glad you've come to live with me."

"And?"

"I'm not gonna contact R.J. He made it clear we had a vacation fling."

"Bawk, bawk, bawk."

"Jeez," Corey muttered. "And you're complaining about me."

"Sounds fair to me," Teague said with a grin.

Corey climbed from his car, locking it once Teague stood on the sidewalk. "What happens if R.J. says no again?"

"What happens if he says yes?" Teague countered.

CHAPTER NINE

COREY ALMOST CHOKED ON the piece of chocolate he was eating when his father strode into the art gallery the next afternoon. Something about his father's stance told him. D-day. His father paused in the imposing entranceway of the gallery, a tall figure posing between marble pillars. He scanned the open floor plan of the gallery, his gaze coming to light on Corey. Lengthy strides brought him to Corey's side in seconds.

They stared at each other. In the past, Corey would have glanced away, shown his submissiveness. Today for some reason he didn't. He caught the brief flare in his father's eyes, the imperceptible flattening of his lips.

Confidence spread in Corey, but he retained enough sense not to gloat. "Did you want something?"

His father crowded him and sniffed, his broad nostrils flaring as he dragged in a breath. "Are you taking the suppression drugs?"

"Of course. It's against the law not to take them."

A frown creased his father's brow. "You smell different."

Corey shrugged, calmly holding his agitated wolf when he wanted to turn tail and flee. "They told us they put an additive in the pills they use to wean off the suppression drugs to make us smell alike. Maybe there's a lingering residue."

"As long as you're taking the pills."

"I'm taking the pills."

His father shot him a steely glare and stepped away. "It's time to stop your silliness, give up chasing a stupid hobby. If you're not at my office tomorrow, ready to work, don't bother coming."

"Pardon?"

"You heard me. If you don't turn up at the office, dressed half decent, you're not welcome at my house or near the pack."

Corey stared, unable to hide his shock. His father was treating him like an errant pack member. "You're threatening me—"

"It's not a threat." His father's phone went off, indicating a text. He fished it from his pocket to read the message. "I'll expect you at nine in the morning. My office. Oh, and Corey, don't try my patience and arrive late." He spun around and stalked out the door before Corey had time to untangle his tongue.

Expulsion.

His father meant to evict him from the pack. This wasn't a warning. He intended to carry out his threat.

"Luv, your father is scary." Gerald minced from the store room, a bright splash of lime green and black against the neutral wall behind their white wooden desk. "I decided I should stay out of your discussion."

Corey had known of Gerald's presence, as had his father.

"What are you going to do, luv? I don't see you in an office."

Neither could he. A problem.

A couple entered the gallery, cutting Gerald's conversation short. They sashayed straight to Gerald when he approached them.

"My brother purchased some paintings of Yellowstone National Park, two days ago. We fell in love with them because they reminded us of our honeymoon. Do you have any similar paintings?"

"As it happens, I know the artist personally," Gerald said smoothly with a meaningful glance at Corey. "If you follow me, we have several paintings available at present. I hope to receive more stock soon."

Yesterday excitement would have pumped through Corey, but right now queasiness roiled in the pit of his stomach, as if someone had kicked him in the gut. His father.

Expulsion from the pack if he didn't follow orders, give up his art. God, he couldn't. Spending hours in an office would hurt. Ignoring his creative urges would feel like cutting off his right arm.

Corey fed the address labels into the printer and started to slap them on envelopes ready for a special newsletter mailing. Part of him liked the mindless task. The other part of him wanted to stop replaying his father's edict and attempting to translate the nuances in the ultimatum.

His father didn't only want him to give up art. He wanted him to quit painting and never pick up a paintbrush again. He wanted another werewolf clone to join his office and make the pack proud.

Corey grabbed the fliers and started to stuff the envelopes. Why had their species changed so radically? Why had they gone underground, never to embrace their heritage? They were like brainless mutts following stupid orders.

Corey continued working, trying to decide what to do with his future, his mind running in ten directions at once.

He placed the last envelope on the pile to post. Aw, hell. He only had one option and he knew it.

Teague ripped his gaze off the small portable television set to accept the cola Corey handed him. "What are you going to do?"

"I've talked to Gerald and handed in my notice. I—"

"Wait! You handed in your notice?"

"Yeah."

"But what are you gonna do?"

Corey stared at the television screen, recalling his father's icy anger in the gallery, the smug certainty his son would follow his orders. A newsflash of the president's visit to neighboring Oregon flickered across the screen. Jeez, he could see more of himself in the president than he could his father. They'd never had a thing in common. It was almost as if his father hated him. "I'm going back to Yellowstone, to see if there's a chance for me and R.J."

"Good for you! Will you give up your apartment?"

"No. I sold two more paintings today. I have plenty to cover the rent. If you wouldn't mind living here, I can leave most of my stuff."

Teague leaned back, his lips quirking up with approval.

"So you're going back to Yellowstone."

"After I talk to my father."

"Your father's scary."

"Try telling me something I don't know." Facing his father would take guts, but he didn't intend to take the coward's way out either. "Would a job in the gallery interest you? I can put in a good word for you."

"Great!"

"Gerald will probably hit on you."

"But he's a decent employer?"

"The best. I'll tell him you're straight when I talk to him."

"How are you gonna handle your father?"

"Not sure yet. I'm not telling him about Yellowstone. I don't want him to make trouble for Hal and R.J."

Corey dragged himself from bed early the next morning, a dull sense of foreboding hitting him from the moment of full awareness.

He popped a suppression pill from a blister pack and swallowed it dry. He needed more pills, yet he'd prevaricated about filling another prescription because the idea of taking the special higher dose pills again, totally subduing his wolf, didn't trip his switch.

And his father had noticed the difference, even if he hadn't clicked as to the cause.

Yet.

He'd need a tight grip on his wolf today. He'd never step into the pack containment area again, if he had his way.

Foregoing his normal makeup, he dressed and headed for the kitchen. One benefit he'd discovered in having a roommate was that the first one up made coffee. He followed the scent to their small kitchen area.

"Gerald said he can see you today and to drop in when you have time."

"Thanks, dude. You okay?"

Damn. "I was hoping my nerves weren't showing."

"They're not. Lucky guess. I'd be shaking if I were in your shoes."

Corey grunted and poured two mugs of coffee. He shunted one at Teague. "Do you want me to drop you at the gallery?"

"Sure, if you have time."

They drove to the gallery in silence, each deep in thought. Unfortunately, the traffic was lighter than usual and Corey reached his father's office building with time to spare.

Oh hell. Taking a deep breath, he swiped his palms down his jeans to dry them. He climbed out of his car and entered the tall glass skyscraper. As usual he reported in at the reception desk. His father didn't welcome visitors wandering around his building. Everyone, even him, suffered an escort to their destination.

"I have an appointment with my father at nine," Corey said.

The attractive blonde behind the reception desk scanned his form rapidly. Her top lip curled a fraction before she spoke into her ear piece. Disdain in one easy glance.

"Mr. Wilson's secretary will come down to accompany you to the top floor. Wait over there."

Corey wandered over to the seating area, picked up a magazine and sat down. He ignored the receptionist's curious gaze and flipped over a page. Instead of reading, Corey stared at the article. He still hadn't decided what he'd say to his father, how he'd tell him art trumped office work every time.

Ten minutes later, the secretary arrived and the man silently led the way to the elevator. He escorted him into his father's office.

The office was a corner one, the two floor-to-ceiling glass walls showcasing spectacular views of the city and the surrounding hills. This office drilled in the truth to those who came to do business. *I am important. I have money and power.*

His father was a snob.

He sat behind his huge wooden desk in an executive chair designed to maintain correct posture. He didn't stand on Corey's entry or invite Corey to sit.

The power play.

Corey came to a halt by the two chairs arranged in front of his father's desk. Comfortable chairs, they were the sort to make the occupant sprawl backward, no matter how straight they attempted to sit. Another subtle power play. Corey remained standing, balancing his weight evenly and waited for his father to speak first.

"I'm pleased you've come to your senses." His expression didn't match his words.

Corey waited for his father's secretary to close the door behind him. "I'm not coming to work for you. I figured I should tell you in person."

Emotion blazed aplenty this time. The dominant one of temper marched across his father's face. "Fuckin' idiot." His hand closed around his gold pen, the distinct crack when it snapped making Corey wince. Half rolled onto his father's desk while the rest dropped to the carpet out of sight.

Corey fought the desire to fidget. "I can't—"

"I mean what I say. If you don't start work today, I will shun you. Your mother will shun you. We won't change our minds."

"I'm sorry you feel that way." Corey swallowed in an attempt to dislodge the lump in his throat. They'd never been close, but he'd never suspected his father hated him. "I'll stop by the house to say goodbye to Mom."

"I'll tell her you've gone." His father picked up a folder and opened it to study the contents in silent dismissal. He produced another gold pen from a drawer and jotted a note on the page.

Shock held Corey rigid. Heat rushed to his face while invisible, icy hands squeezed his chest. He hesitated a fraction longer before turning for the door.

Total commitment to his art was his dream and the ability to do this should've thrilled him. Instead, his father had stolen the victory away from him.

⇢⇢⇢ ⇠⇠⇠

"You don't have to come with me to the airport."

"I'm your friend," Teague said gruffly. "Besides, you've done a lot for me."

Corey shrugged, uncomfortable at the sentiments. "I'm letting you stay in my apartment and drive my car. Big deal."

"Thanks to you I have a part-time job. Gerald said one of his friends might have a job for me at his restaurant."

"Gerald's a great guy if you can get past his weird outfits and outlandish behavior."

"You were good training." Teague's grin held a hint of sly. "I remember the way you looked when you arrived at Yellowstone. Stark black with a pudgy white face."

"I never had a pudgy face."

"Did too."

Corey chuckled at the ridiculous conversation. At least he possessed friends even if his family and pack shunned him. "Do you mind if we drive past my parents' house before we hit the airport? I can't leave without saying goodbye to my mom."

"It's your car."

"Yours now. Use it as much as you want."

"Thanks, Corey. I appreciate your generosity."

"Shut up," Corey said. "You don't owe me anything." Teague's presence had helped him to keep sane since their return from Yellowstone. If anything, he owed Teague.

The surroundings grew more luxurious, the houses larger and more imposing and the vehicles more expensive as they neared his parents' house.

Teague whistled when Corey pulled up in front of gold gilded gates. "I still can't get over this house. Some digs."

"Yeah." Teague wouldn't understand how lonely he'd been as a child, despite the large number of staff. "I'll leave the car out here in case my father is home. He should be at work by now but you never know." Without waiting for Teague's reply, he climbed out of the car and hurried to the small side entrance gate. He pushed several numbers on the keypad, part of him surprised when his code still worked. The gate clicked shut behind him, the loud clack making him start. His heart battered his ribs in a rapid tattoo and a nervous laugh emerged.

Weird. Not a single bird chirped.

The instant the thought registered, he paused and sniffed. A familiar scent filled his nostrils and lungs. He sniffed again to make sure. This time he proceeded with caution, gliding into the undergrowth instead of taking the winding path leading directly to the front door.

The scent of wolf smelled stronger here. Corey cautiously peered through a gap in the foliage of a bush. His heart practically forced itself up his throat.

Enforcers. Three of them.

He ducked down, making himself small.

Were they here for him? Would his father really throw him to the wolves?

The static of a radio reached him. "No, nothing here. I'm going to send Rick to man the entrance gate."

Stealthily, Corey backed away. Once out of sight, he hurried through the undergrowth. Soon, someone would realize he'd punched in his code, if they hadn't already. He picked up his pace, yet took care with his footing, racing adjacent to the path, not wanting the crunch of gravel underfoot to give him away.

Once at the gate, he flung it open, thankful he didn't need to punch in a code this side of the fence. Seconds later he wrenched open the driver's door and jumped inside his car.

"What's wrong?"

"Enforcers." Corey didn't waste another breath. He peeled away from the curb, fear prodding him to speed. He didn't understand why Enforcers guarded the house, but given the way he and his father parted, he didn't intend to confront them and ask questions.

Chapter Ten

He missed him. Badly.

Corey's absence ached like a broken bone during a cold snap. An image of Corey's face, the hurt and the betrayal, stained his memories. The vision turned into an accusing nightmare, stalking him whenever he dozed. *A good fuck.* The words echoed through his mind in a taunting litany.

The truth, but what he'd failed to add was the way Corey claimed his heart. He missed him.

"R.J.? What is wrong with you?" Hal's abrupt demand broke through his tortured thoughts.

R.J. focused on his untouched meal. His stomach churned like the Yellowstone river rapids. He tossed his knife and fork down, unable to eat. Every mouthful tasted about as appetizing as frozen winter grass anyway.

"R.J.?" This time Hal grasped his shoulder and tugged for good measure. "I've been talking to myself for five minutes."

"Sorry, what did you say?"

"I was telling you about my cousins who arrive tomorrow."

"So soon?"

"Yes."

R.J. forced his mind to practicalities. "How long are they visiting?"

"A few days." Hal's gaze drilled into R.J., concern creating a frown. "Are you sure there's nothing bothering you?"

"Nothing I can't fix."

"You'll need to keep your wits about you while my relations are here."

"Why? Are they rabid?"

"I want to make sure they stay out of trouble. That we stay out of trouble."

It was R.J.'s turn to frown. "I won't let you down. You can count on me. I'll do everything in my power to make sure your cousins have a good time while they're here."

"As long as we don't have any surprise admin visits from the board."

"Hell, don't even think it," R.J. warned. "One visit a year

is more than enough." He stood, grabbing Hal's empty plate and the remains of his meal to carry out to the kitchen. "I haven't been sleeping well. I might have an early night."

"We'll need to discuss the next intake of students tomorrow. Decide on which ones to admit and work out if we can fit in another scholarship student."

"Sure. What time do your cousins arrive?"

"In the afternoon, assuming they make the connecting flights."

"Do you want to sort out the intake tomorrow morning then?"

"Works for me."

The next afternoon Hal jumped every time the wind rattled through the tree outside his office. R.J. would have laughed, but he wasn't in much better condition.

"I'm going for a run," he said. "You don't need me, right?"

"Go ahead."

"We haven't utilized the area over to the west. I want to explore, see if it's suitable to use for some of our classes."

Hal nodded. "See you later."

R.J. drove and parked his vehicle at the end of the track. This time he chose an arduous route, one he knew most casual human tourists would consider twice before choosing. Once he'd trekked out of sight of the parking area, he scrutinized his surroundings, testing the air twice to make certain he was alone.

When nothing except the chatter of a curious chipmunk disturbed the peace, he set down his day pack and whipped off his clothes. After stuffing them into his pack, he put it plus his boots under a bush, camouflaging both with dried leaves.

The air brushed across his naked skin like a caress. Unfortunately, the whisper-soft stroke reminded him of Corey. Everything reminded him of Corey. The kid plain haunted him, or perhaps it was his guilty conscience.

R.J. called up his wolf, embracing the shift before he raced through the forest, attempting to outrun his demons.

THE ENFORCERS RATTLED COREY big time. At the last minute, he'd purchased a ticket to New York rather than flying to an airport near Yellowstone.

Personally, Teague thought he'd overreacted, but his friend could afford the eccentricity. Teague couldn't. Since Corey's departure, he'd filled his day with job interviews and work at the gallery.

Corey had spoken the truth about the gallery. Gerald was a good employer despite his flamboyant ways. Thanks to his new boss, this morning he'd scored a job waiting tables at a popular Italian restaurant. While the wages weren't great, the place was trendy and booked solid and the tips would swell his savings. He didn't give a rat's ass for fashion or trends, but if they helped him provide for his mother and brothers he was in favor of exclusivity.

With plenty of time to spare, he dressed in black trousers and the shirt provided by the restaurant.

A thump on his apartment door brought a scowl. No one knew he lived there, apart from Gerald. A casual visitor shouldn't have made it past the doorman and the security door below.

He hesitated and sniffed. Even with the suppression drugs, he sensed wolf.

Shit. He delayed even longer before grimacing. This was stupid. He hadn't done anything wrong. He padded from the bedroom out into the hall. Another series of thumps echoed and made the door jump on its hinges.

"Hang on!" He peered through the security spy hole.

Two big men flanked a man in an expensive business suit. When they moved, he recognized Corey's father. A third even bigger man stood close to his door. Obviously the one who'd threatened to beat his door down. Hell, this did not look good.

Swallowing down his trepidation, he opened the door.

"Where's Corey?" Corey's father came straight to the point. The man didn't look much like his son. He'd thought the same the other night.

"Corey went to New York." Despite himself, a tremor crept into his voice. Those three dudes looked scary.

"New York?" Corey's father's gaze sliced and diced, leaving Teague full of foreboding. Aw, fuck. He didn't believe him.

"Yeah, I dropped him off at the airport a few days ago. I—" He broke off deciding to stick to scant facts.

"I what?"

"I was gonna say I haven't heard from him."

"What's he doing in New York?"

"Job hunting, I think." Teague found himself crumbling under the harsh glare from Corey's father. "He wanted to pursue his art."

Corey's father lifted a brow and fear writhed inside Teague. Fuck. Corey was right to worry about his father. Not paranoid at all. The man didn't bear an ounce of affection for his son, not one that showed on his face. And what sort of parent took along three big goons for protection when he wanted information about his son? Didn't bode well, not for him or Corey.

"Where in New York?"

"I don't know."

"You're lying." Corey's father flicked a glance in the direction of the nearest goon. "Bring him with us. We'll get answers one way or another."

The goon pounced before Teague could react or try to duck. He didn't see the fist coming until it struck his face.

MOST PEOPLE WOULD CALL him paranoid. Teague hadn't believed him or understood his concern once he'd seen the Enforcers. Corey trusted his instincts, which meant taking the long way back to Yellowstone, starting with a flight to New York and a combination of planes, trains and buses to reach his final destination. He didn't want to create problems for R.J.

Know thine enemy. It was a theory his father subscribed to in his pack and business dealings. To Corey, the presence of the Enforcers at the family home indicated something nefarious and he intended to act with caution.

The tour bus pulled up at the park entrance and the tour guide took care of the admission fee. Finally, after zigzagging all over the country, he was arriving back at Yellowstone.

And, for the first time in his life, he'd dressed to blend and appear like an average tourist. He stared down at his faded blue jeans and his white button-down shirt, the emblem of a New York baseball team on the pocket. He'd teamed them with a new pair of sturdy boots, a cap and a pair of dark sunglasses. The cap helped cover his hair, which was still an unnatural black after his last dye job. R.J. would probably chuckle when he saw him, if he wasn't too pissed with Corey for turning up unannounced.

His hair would lose its color once he had an opportunity to shift—

Corey slammed the brakes on his thoughts, a shocked gasp emerging. Treason. That was treason. Shifting without possessing formal paperwork was illegal, punishable by death. Yet the forbidden called him, the idea of running across the land seductive and appealing.

"Can you see something?" the tourist sitting beside him demanded. "An animal? I want to see a wolf. Did you see a wolf?"

"No, I thought of something I forgot to do." He wanted to see a wolf too. Somehow he didn't think they had the same beast in mind.

"Oh," the Austrian said. "You should concentrate on the scenery. You might miss something."

Up ahead, the tour guide broke in on her spiel about

the history of the park to point out a herd of bison. Immediately everyone craned their necks in the direction she pointed. Cameras clicked and whirred and the three children near him jumped up and down, letting out piercing shrieks of excitement. Corey winced and he wasn't the only one.

"Can I get past?" the Austrian asked. "I'd like to take a photo."

"There are some on this side," Corey said, pointing.

"Where?"

"To the right of those two rocks. See them?" Crap, he'd forgotten his eyesight was better than average. The drugs in his system weren't doing much to dim his wolfish senses.

"Where? Oh! I think I see them. You have good eyesight."

"My mother made me eat lots of carrots," Corey said. The man wasn't listening, too busy fiddling with his camera.

Corey sat impatiently through the many photo stops on the way to Old Faithful and the point at which he intended to leave the tour. Finally, they arrived. Corey collected his bag of art materials and waited for everyone else to rush off before he had a quiet word with the tour guide.

"I've decided I'd like to spend longer here than a day."

"We don't give refunds," the tour guide said in a sharp

voice.

"I don't require a refund," Corey said. "I didn't realize how much there was to see. Is there a phone number I can call to book a place on a tour bus out of here?"

Slightly mollified, the tour guide gave him a business card.

"Thanks," Corey said and walked off, excitement bubbling like a thermal mud pool inside him. He couldn't wait to see R.J.

First, he took care of business, dropping by to check in with the places he'd left his artwork.

"Corey!" The manager of the first shop greeted him in delight. "Have you brought more paintings? I sold out in a few days."

"I have two." He handed them over, slightly embarrassed when she praised them so highly. Apart from Gerald and his friends here, everyone in his life treated his interest in art with indulgence. "I haven't had time to do more."

"Make time," the woman ordered. "I can sell them." She wrote him a check and handed it over. Corey stared at the amount for a moment, stunned because for once in his life he possessed more money than he could spend. It gave him independence, options.

"What's the easiest way to get to Tower-Roosevelt village?" Corey asked.

"If you don't mind waiting, I can give you a ride later tonight," the woman said. "I want to check the stock in the shop up there."

"I'm meeting a friend," Corey said. "I'd hoped to get there by this afternoon." The impatient push from his wolf confirmed the urgency thrumming through him. He wanted to run through the forest as much as he wanted to eyeball R.J.

"A woman?"

Corey shrugged at the flirtatious smile. "Yes," he said without blinking. R.J. would be amused to learn he'd suddenly changed sex.

"Ah well. Can't win them all. I still want more pictures, young man."

"Thanks."

"You might catch a ride with Melvin. I think his next delivery is in that direction."

The doorbell tinkled and a large bear of a man pushed through carrying a box of fresh fruit. "I have more to unload. Do you want me to come through the side door?"

"Please," the woman said. "Corey needs a ride to Tower. Do you have room for him?"

Melvin considered Corey. "You're not a chatterbox?"

"No, sir."

"Corey is an artist. He painted that picture of

Yellowstone you liked."

"You're welcome to a ride," Melvin said.

"I can help you unload," Corey said. Anything to reach R.J.

R.J. arrived back from yet another run, physically tired yet wired at the same time. None of the activity killed his yearning for Corey. If anything, the longing was worse.

He rushed at his cabin door and almost flattened his nose when the door didn't give. Damn. Locked. The werewolf fugitives were a suspicious lot.

Next week a group of students were arriving so they wouldn't have any relatives staying again until the students departed for home.

"It's R.J.," he said in a gruff voice. "You going to let me in?"

The door cracked open a scant inch.

"It's me," R.J. repeated impatiently. Part of him understood the need for caution. But the insight didn't soothe his short-tempered wolf that missed Corey and didn't understand why they couldn't stay together.

The door opened another inch, far enough for R.J. to see the blonde woman on the other side. "You're a pain in the ass."

"A live pain," the woman said, opening the door only after she'd scanned the vicinity again. "Being neurotic helps me stay alive."

"Maybe, but it's a hell of a way to live."

She shut the door behind him and turned the lock with a loud click. "You smell."

"Thanks for the compliment."

She cocked her head. "Sarcasm? Why? It's the truth. You stink."

"That's why I'm here, to get my stuff for a shower."

They both heard footsteps outside seconds before someone rapped on the door.

"Who is it?" Emma's words were scarcely audible.

"Probably Hal." R.J. moved toward the door.

"Hey, R.J., you in there?"

Corey? Ignoring Emma's protest, R.J. unlocked the door and yanked it open. He stared at Corey for an instant, uncertain of how to react. God, he wasn't dreaming. "Corey, what are you doing here?" Hell, that hadn't come out the way he meant it to. He dragged Corey inside and slammed the door. The next instant he hauled Corey into his arms and kissed him. Their noses clashed and his teeth mashed against Corey's bottom lip. Instinctively, he softened the contact and their connection flowed through him in a soothing wave.

Corey was here. He didn't know how or why. Didn't care. All he wanted to do was kiss him, hold him.

SHELLEY MUNRO

When they finally parted, they were both breathing hard.

"Are you pleased to see me?" Corey gripped his shoulders, seemingly unable to release him. Not that it worried R.J. "I thought you'd tell me to piss off."

"Well that was enlightening," Emma said.

Every muscle in Corey's body tensed. "You have a woman in your cabin."

R.J. ignored Emma's roll of the eyes to focus on Corey. He couldn't tell him the truth. It wasn't his place for a start. "Emma is Hal's cousin. She's staying here for a couple of days."

"Why is she in your cabin? There are others."

Part of R.J. enjoyed Corey's jealousy. The other part recognized Corey's presence brought problems for all of them. He'd have to explain things to Hal. Emma wouldn't keep what she'd seen quiet.

"You're not together?" Corey's confidence faltered and R.J.'s heart twisted at the pain in his voice.

Emma sniffed. "Do you think he'd kiss you like that if he was interested in me? If he and I were involved and I witnessed him kiss someone else like he kissed you I'd bash him over the head."

"I wouldn't spend time with a viper-mouth like you if someone paid me to," R.J. snapped.

194

"Ah, but someone *is* paying you," Emma retorted sweetly.

Corey looked confused. "Huh?"

R.J. ignored Emma. "What are you doing here?"

"Aren't you glad to see me?"

"Yes. Very glad, but why are you here?"

"I couldn't stop thinking about you." Corey paused and bit his bottom lip in obvious indecision.

"And?"

"My father told me to make a decision. Work for him or art. I chose art."

"Doesn't explain why you're here." He hated the words emerging from his mouth, the harsh tone, but he needed to ask the tough questions. Other people relied on him to help keep them safe. Hal counted on him.

And he owed Hal big time.

Corey swallowed. He looked different. Younger. Too young for him, R.J.'s conscience taunted him. The eight years between them might as well be a lifetime.

"My father kicked me out of the pack." A tremor shook him, and for a second, R.J. thought he might cry.

"Aw, fuck. Corey, I'm sorry." Seeing the misery in Corey's face made him forget Emma's presence. He stepped close again and hauled the kid into his arms. The contact seemed to soothe Corey's trembling. It certainly pacified R.J.'s agitated wolf. "Are you still taking suppression drugs?"

"Yeah."

"When did you take your last one?"

Surprise darted across Corey's face. "This morning."

"Does your father realize you're here?" *Does he know about me?*

"No. I flew to New York first and made my way here gradually."

"Why would you do that?" Emma demanded.

"Because my father is a control freak. He'd take pleasure in seeing me fail, and I didn't want to give him the opportunity."

Maybe this wouldn't be the big problem R.J. envisaged. "Does anyone know you're here?"

"Only Teague. He was rooming with me."

A flash of jealousy shot through R.J. "Teague."

"We're friends. He needed somewhere to live and I like him. He's good company."

R.J. let his breath ease out. "Okay." He shot a swift glance at Emma. "I need to talk to Hal."

"I'll come with you."

"No, you'd better stay here with Emma."

"Why?"

"I'll explain later." *Please let him follow the suggestion.*

R.J. worried about the conversation ahead. Hal was jumpy enough with the werewolves around. Corey's presence was a complication they didn't need.

R.J. headed straight for Hal's office. He rapped on the door.

"Hal, there's a problem."

"What?"

"Corey Wilson has turned up."

Clear horror shot across Hal's face, followed by a scowl. "Why?"

R.J. explained.

"Fuck! Why now?" His eyes narrowed and R.J. fought the need to shift his weight from foot to foot. "What aren't you telling me?"

"Corey and I..." R.J. trailed off, panic surging through him. If he lost this job or Hal's respect he'd have nothing.

CHAPTER ELEVEN

COREY STARED AT EMMA, struggling to keep his jealousy from morphing into words that might haunt him at a future date. He might have feelings for R.J. but they weren't returned. Their earlier kiss didn't prove anything apart from sexual attraction.

His youth and inexperience crowded in on him, creating a knee-weakening surge of self-doubt. Yet he wouldn't change anything he'd done to date. He refused to apologize for his actions.

"Look at you, kid," Emma said, breaking into his mental agonizing, her mocking smile filling him with foreboding. "You've got the man in a tangle. You have power and you're wasting it away."

And she was a smart-ass, poking her nose in where she

had no business. "Who are you? And why are you sharing a cabin with R.J.?"

"Why do *you* think I'm sharing a cabin with R.J.?"

Corey glanced at the rumpled beds. "Not for sex."

"You sure about that?" A mocking smile flashed again, but it didn't reach her eyes or cancel out the smart-ass sneer that seemed like her pre-set expression.

"R.J. didn't shrink from kissing me in front of you. There are two beds in here. R.J.'s is tidy while yours shows signs of recent use." Corey sniffed, knowledge blooming though him when his senses registered something else. "And your scent is nothing like R.J.'s. You're not taking the suppression drugs and I'd guess you're an unregistered wolf."

"Quite the little detective, aren't you?" She took half a step toward him, a fluid prowl intended to intimidate.

Corey didn't move, not even a flinch. "There's no need to threaten me. I'm not a blabbermouth."

Her eyes narrowed in contemplation, head cocking to the side like an inquisitive bird. "I think I like you."

"Yeah?" Corey gestured at her claws, clearly visible beyond the short, clipped fingernails. "You might want to put those back where they came from."

The cabin door flew open, bouncing against the doorjamb with a loud crash. R.J. loomed in the doorway.

"I'm glad to see you're getting along well. I could hear you from outside. You won't hurt him."

"Chill. I have no intention of hurting him," Emma said. "Besides, he doesn't need you to baby him. He's doing fine on his own."

Corey spied Hal standing behind R.J. A frown furrowed the older man's brow, his worry clear for anyone who studied body language. Was it his return to Yellowstone or something else? "Have I come at a bad time?"

"You might say that," Emma said. "You guys going to come inside or do you want to attract curiosity from the day-trippers stopping by to book for the wildlife program?"

R.J. shot her a glare of dislike but stepped inside, away from the doorway, to let his boss into the cabin. Hal shut the door, making the interior shrink.

"Corey," Hal said. "It's good to see you again."

Emma cocked her head, intelligence glinting in her dark eyes. "You're not telling the truth. Why don't they want you here, kid? You don't smell dangerous."

"Why does everyone have to call me kid?"

"Because you're young." Emma cast one of her mocking smirks at R.J. "Maybe not so innocent."

"Corey, if you don't mind sharing a cabin, there's a spare

bed in the one you stayed in last time," Hal said. "Come and see me in my office once you get set. We need to talk."

Hal and R.J. exchanged a glance that shot a bundle of nerves into Corey's stomach. "I'll dump my bag and head straight over to your office."

"Only one bag?" Hal asked.

R.J. barked out a laugh.

Heat filled Corey's cheeks. He deserved it. He'd behaved like a little shit on his arrival last time. "Just the one bag. I'm traveling light with one change of clothes and my art supplies."

"Last time Corey visited he brought four bags," Hal told Emma.

Her full lips quivered. "City boy, huh?"

Corey rolled his eyes and pushed past R.J. to get to the door. "Won't be long."

He stooped to pick up his bag and headed for cabin six. If they forced him to leave, he didn't know what he'd do, not with his limited options. Go back to Los Angeles or start afresh somewhere else. Neither option struck him as palatable. At least they weren't kicking him out right away. The fact eased some of his anxiety and his mood improved. If Hal didn't want him there, he wouldn't have offered him the use of a cabin.

Ten minutes later, he knocked on Hal's office door. Hal

and R.J. were already present.

"R.J. told me about your affair," Hal said, getting straight to the point.

"Is R.J. in trouble? The last thing I want is for him to lose his job," Corey said. "I'll leave if that's the case."

"You haven't arrived at a good time," Hal said. "Did your father approve of you coming here?"

"He doesn't know I've left Los Angeles."

"He'll want to find you and won't have any trouble tracking you," Hal said with certainty.

Corey frowned in confusion. Why would it matter? "My father gave me an ultimatum. Work for him or leave the pack. I decided to leave." Corey's scowl deepened when he remembered trying to say goodbye to his mother. The Enforcers' presence wasn't for a tea party. Their watchful attitudes indicated that. Not careful enough though. If they'd been waiting for him, they'd made a mistake in assuming him a naïve city kid. The label would have fit before he'd attended the Yellowstone camp. R.J. and Hal had taught him a lot. "I purchased a ticket to New York and flew there before making my way back to Yellowstone by a combination of bus and planes."

"Why did you do that?" Hal's tone was sharp.

"Instinct. I stopped by to see my mother and the presence of Enforcers worried me. I decided some of the rumors I've heard might have merit. It was a gut thing."

Hal straightened abruptly. "What did the Enforcers want?"

"Did they see you?" R.J. asked, his brow furrowing.

"I didn't approach the house in my normal manner. Something told me not to so I followed my instincts. When I saw them I decided to forget a visit." Corey hesitated, wondering whether to tell them about his wolf and the suppression pills. Since being back in Yellowstone, he'd sensed his wolf even stronger than he'd felt him in L.A. The tablets they'd given him didn't work any longer. Despite taking a pill this morning, he thought he could shift to wolf now without difficulty.

"Anything else?" R.J. asked.

"The suppression pills don't work for me."

Hal's mouth dropped open in astonishment while R.J. stared, an unfathomable expression on his face.

"What? How?" Hal asked finally.

Because he was a freak. Corey shrugged. "How should I know?"

"Who knows about this?"

"When did you take your last pill?"

The questions flew quick and fast.

"My father knows and the doctors and scientists in the pack's underground lab. I told you I took a pill this morning."

"Start from the beginning, Corey," Hal said. "Don't leave a thing out."

"At first the pills worked. I started taking them when I was around five, the age when parents register their offspring. When I turned fourteen, I started butting heads with my father. I wanted to take art courses instead of the classes he wanted me to take in accounting and technical drawing."

"Go on," Hal said.

"One day I lost my temper with my father. He'd forbidden me to take an art course and I was so angry..." Corey trailed off, recalling his fury at his father's edict. He refused to let him study to learn portraiture from one of the best artists on the West Coast. A vein twitched at his temple and renewed anger surged through him. When it came to his art, his father was intractable.

"Corey, tell us what happened," R.J. said.

A noticeable shiver racked Corey and R.J. moved closer, gripping his shoulder in silent encouragement.

"I didn't change properly. I transformed halfway and got stuck. I couldn't finish the change and I didn't know how to shift back to human. I freaked. In the end they locked me away in the cells below the pack buildings. The doctors and scientists poked and prodded me and gradually I returned to human form. After that my father made sure I received a higher dosage of the suppression pills. Until I went off the pills here I couldn't sense my wolf at all."

Hal frowned. "Did your father tell anyone? And why would he risk sending you on the course here?"

"I wondered myself, but my father wouldn't like others knowing about a weakness in his son," Corey said. "I doubt he told anyone because no one bothered me after he got me out of the cells. Whenever I run out of pills I go to my father for a script. He told me to fill it at a small pharmacy near Chinatown." Corey's throat moved in an audible swallow, recalling the agonized screams he'd heard while incarcerated in the cells. Once he'd heard Enforcers beating some unlucky prick in the cell next to him. The crunch of fist against flesh and bone was a sound he never wanted to hear again.

"And the course?"

"That's easier to answer," R.J. said. "As head of the pack, he'd want the prestige of his son going on the course. It's a subtle power play to show his strength and status."

"Yep, my father is all about status and appearing powerful," Corey said. "It's that simple, plus he wanted me out of the way while he held negotiations with a neighboring pack. My failure to behave in a manner he deems proper embarrasses him."

Hal nodded. "And coming here was low risk because all of the kids go off the suppression pills."

"Exactly," R.J. said.

"It's time for us to go for a run. Emma and the others will welcome the exercise," Hal said, changing the subject. "Corey, we need you to keep away from the dining area and the other public areas unless you wear a hat and make yourself appear like a tourist. I'd appreciate it if you didn't contact anyone at home."

"All right." Curiosity rose in Corey. All this secrecy was obviously something to do with Emma. And Hal had mentioned other wolves. He decided to observe instead of asking questions. Only Teague knew his location and he wouldn't tattle.

Hal disappeared, leaving them alone. R.J. closed the door and turned to face him, leaning his weight against the hard wood.

Corey bit his lip. "Have I landed you in trouble?"

"You haven't exactly made things easy for me."

"I'm sorry." His gaze slid away from R.J.'s as shame filled him. Once again he'd jumped in with both feet instead of thinking. He'd missed R.J. so bad.

"Corey?"

"Yeah?" Corey swallowed, bracing himself for a

rejection.

"I missed you. A lot. I'm glad you came back because I hated the way we parted. I've kicked myself ever since you left. I wanted to call you."

"Really?" Relief made him dizzy.

"Yeah. Now shut up and kiss me quick before Hal comes back."

Corey flew into R.J.'s arms. Their lips met and Corey put every wayward emotion into the kiss. His desire. His liking for R.J. and the fact he'd missed him dreadfully. Yearning crashed through him, a whimper of pleasure escaping. His hands mapped R.J.'s broad shoulders and he clung while their lips mated and their tongues tangled with enthusiasm.

The kiss proved one thing. His memories didn't do their passion justice. He'd been right to return. Hopefully R.J. felt the same way.

Corey gripped R.J. tighter and kissed him, groaning in disapproval when R.J. lifted his head and pushed him away.

"Why did you stop?"

"Hal will return in a minute. Knowing about us and witnessing the fact are two different things."

Chagrin flooded Corey. He'd made things worse for R.J. "I'm sorry."

"Hey, don't apologize. Normally your arrival wouldn't cause problems."

"I should have called first, but all I could think about was seeing you again."

"And getting away from your father."

Corey grimaced. "That too. I was careful. I doubt my father will search for me. He doesn't like me and nothing I do is ever good enough for him."

"Blood ties don't make a family."

"Ain't that the truth." Corey thought back to his childhood. His father hadn't always worked this hard, yet he'd never spent time with him either. His friends' parents played with them, took them out to the fun parks and for dinner. Corey couldn't remember a single time when his father took him on an outing. His mother had taken him to the beach, to the movies and to play with other kids. Never his father. Funny, he hadn't considered it strange until now.

Only his loss of temper and partial shift had grabbed his father's attention. And, recently his refusal to work with him.

Hal returned and R.J.'s hands dropped from Corey's shoulders. "You ready to go?"

"We'll take the bus. People are used to seeing us with people in a bus and the ones here for the season won't notice or suspect anything different."

"Good idea. Corey, you know where we keep the water. Grab seven for us."

"Seven?"

"We'll answer your questions later." R.J. waited for Corey's nod of acquiescence before leaving him alone with Hal.

Corey gnawed on his bottom lip, acknowledging his worry—the worry he should have considered before arriving on their doorstep. "Will my presence cause trouble for you?"

"I honestly don't know. You told us everything?"

"Yes."

"Don't worry," Hal said. "I'll see you in a few minutes out the front."

Corey was the last to board the bus, lugging the requested water. Three men and Emma sat at the front of the bus, just behind Hal and R.J.

"How do we know we can trust him?" one of the men said.

The other two glared at Corey, faces filled with menacing agreement.

"I think he's kinda cute," Emma drawled.

Corey opened his mouth and shut it again. Silence might be his best option at this stage. He'd bulked out during the last three months but he wouldn't have a chance against these men.

"Where does he come from? What is he doing here?" the man persisted. His dark eyes glinted with distrust.

"I told you before. He's one of our students," Hal said, his sharp tone telling Corey he'd repeated the words several times already.

Time for Corey to speak. "I come from Los Angeles. I'm an artist. I came to visit R.J. and to check in on the store and the two lodges that are stocking my paintings on consignment. They want more paintings so I intend to stay and paint."

His words stopped the growling and the muttering although the men still shot him looks full of suspicion. Corey wanted to ask questions of his own.

"What's your name, kid?" Emma asked.

"Corey."

"Corey who? You have another name, right?"

The woman had a real attitude. Corey's glowered at her. "Yes, I have another name."

Emma flashed a white grin at him. Unrepentant. "Well, what is it? Are you ashamed of your name?"

"Corey Wilson." Most people knew his father or had at least heard of him. He took a deep breath and waited for the fallout.

"Wilson," one of the men snarled.

"Yes."

"Relation to Grant?"

Corey didn't say anything. He didn't have to since the answer was written over his face.

"Fuck, I thought this was a fuckin' safe house," the nearest man snarled. "We have to leave. Now." He stood, taking two giant steps toward the exit door before Hal reached over and seized his arm.

"Don't be stupid," Hal said. "I explained everything to you."

"You didn't tell us his name," Emma snapped.

"You're only here for three more nights. Corey's father doesn't realize he's here."

The men continued to glare, and Corey hurriedly changed the subject. "Where are we going? This is a different way than we used to go for our lessons."

"We like to vary our days. It's not good for wolf sightings to take place in the same areas all the time," R.J. said.

"A run will do us good," Hal said. "Get rid of some of the stored energy and nerves."

"Is he here to guard the bus?" Emma asked.

"Not exactly," Hal said.

R.J. pulled into a side road Corey hadn't noticed before. The road was narrow and bumpy, tree branches scraped the windows and body of the bus as they passed.

Corey's teeth rattled and if he hadn't grabbed the seat in front, he would have fallen to the floor. One of the men cursed.

Another shouted, "R.J., where did you get your license? In a cereal box?"

Emma laughed, wildness in her eyes, and Corey couldn't help but grin back. The insults about R.J.'s driving flew hard and fast with R.J. flinging verbal abuse right back. The joking lightened the atmosphere and a much happier group exited the bus at the end of the track.

R.J. led the way to a winding path, not much bigger than a goat trail. Corey inhaled deeply and caught a whiff of deer, animals that passed this way a few hours earlier. He noticed the blades of grass and a freshly broken twig on an overhanging branch. Stepping carefully he avoided the pile of droppings. He took in these things automatically, delighting in the smells and sounds of the forest. After the closeness of the city and the multitude of sweaty bodies, the fresh crisp tang of the forest hit him like a health tonic.

"This looks familiar," he said to R.J.

"We didn't range this far during our training, but you might have come this way during your hunt."

"Do you have to chatter like a couple of raucous birds?" Emma demanded. "I want to hunt today."

"I'm sorry." Corey understood the urge to run in wolf form. A thought occurred, one so obvious he was surprised he hadn't thought of it earlier. These people weren't students, and only students qualified for the summer program at Yellowstone, which meant...

"We'll leave our stuff here," R.J. said. "There's a space behind this pile of rocks to hide our gear. I've left clothing here before."

They stashed their packs and moved back.

R.J. grinned at him. "Corey, I'll race you to shift."

Corey started to fling off his clothes, the chance to best R.J. too good to pass. He laughed out loud at R.J.'s ripe curse. "Should remove the boots first." A cackle of delight escaped him, his breathing coming fast as the urgent desire to win poured adrenaline through his veins.

A clear rip of fabric rent the air when he tore his boxer-briefs down his legs. Free of his clothes, he visualized his wolf, embracing the pain and the distinct pleasure of the shift. His wolf rolled over him, his bones cracking and reshaping, fur sprouting across his naked skin. He fell forward onto all fours and seconds later, his wolfish senses burst upon him.

In his wolf form he turned to see R.J. His lover stood beside Hal, naked, but not attempting to shift.

"It's true," Hal said. "He can shift even though he's

taking the suppression pills."

Astonished, Corey sat on his haunches instead of bursting into a sprint as he'd originally intended. Hal was right, and he didn't feel any different now from when he'd gone off the pills and shifted.

The pills really didn't work!

The implications brought a tremble and he slunk across the ground to R.J., seeking comfort. As he had when he'd changed the first time, R.J. crouched beside him and petted him until his quivering stopped.

"Does anyone know about this?" one of the men demanded.

"Corey's father," Hal answered.

Emma scowled at Corey before turning her glower on Hal. "He hid it?"

Corey couldn't decide if their anger was directed at him or his father.

Hal shook his head. "Not exactly. He let the doctors and scientists use his son as a test subject."

"How did he get free?" another of the men asked.

"His father got the doctors to formulate stronger pills for him."

"So why has he changed now?"

"We gave Corey a supply of pills when he left Yellowstone. We give all the kids a fresh supply of pills when they leave. I'd say he's watched Corey and waited for any signs of his wolf to appear," R.J. said.

To Corey's relief R.J. continued the physical contact, scratching him and ruffling his fur. He sidled closer until he pressed against R.J.'s naked thigh. He listened closely, yet didn't feel the need to join in the conversation. It was interesting—the ramifications. He'd never thought of his father's behavior in this light before. Why had he let the doctors and scientists poke and prod him then let him free?

That part didn't make sense. It wasn't as if he and his father got along.

"Why didn't Wilson make sure his son took the stronger pills?" one of the men asked.

"I don't know. Perhaps he thought it a passing phase. For all we know he might be keeping a close eye on his son, waiting to see what happens," Hal said.

There was an edgy pause, the snarls emanating from one of the men scaring Corey. His hackles rose and he returned a growl, despite his fear. This wasn't his fault, dammit.

"What if he wants his son back?" one of the men demanded, a threatening edge to his voice.

When R.J. stretched to his full height to face the threat, Corey sidled behind him.

"Or if he's tracked his son here?" another asked.

SHELLEY MUNRO

"Putting us all in danger," Emma finished, summing up their thoughts.

"Crap," one of the men said. "We need to check him for tracking devices."

Emma went to Corey's day pack and rifled through the compartments. "Does he have a cell phone?"

"No," R.J. said. "At least he didn't during his last visit. Corey doesn't like them. Said he didn't like making it easy for his father to contact him. The other kids had one each but not Corey."

"That's good news," Hal said. "It also means they didn't put any tracking devices on his body when they had him in the med labs."

"Any shifting would upset a tracking device," R.J. said. "If they'd injected one under his skin, the number of shifts he's done would've destroyed it by now."

"Makes sense," one of the men grudgingly agreed. The tension leached from his body. "We'll check his belongings in case he's brought a tracking device with him."

Corey didn't see how. None of his belongings had been anywhere near his father. In fact, several items were new, purchased in New York to help his disguise. The only things he'd brought with him from Los Angeles were art supplies.

"Do we need to do it right now?" Emma pouted, but her

sulk didn't look pretty or enticing. She looked downright scary. "I wanted a run. I'm going to crazy if I don't run. *Today.*"

"R.J., Corey and I will go back to the camp," Hal said finally. "You guys take a run and either R.J. or I will come and pick you up once we're assured of your safety. Meanwhile we'll go through Corey's stuff and search for anything suspicious."

"How do we know you'll do a good job?" one of the men asked.

Fuck, they were a trusting lot. Corey came out from behind R.J. He shifted back to human and grabbed his scattered clothes. He'd looked forward to a run—didn't look as if he'd get one today.

R.J. glared and took half a step toward the man. "Hal and I are putting our lives on the line to help you. Why the fuck would we sabotage ourselves?"

One of the others grabbed the man's arm and hauled him back.

"They're right. We have to trust them." He turned to Hal. "Do you think we can move things along? Move us to the next safe house sooner than scheduled."

"Good suggestion," Hal said. "I'll contact the major, let him know we have a problem."

The man gave a curt nod. "That'll work. If the worst

happens, we can always hole up out here. We've slept rough before."

"We'll leave our water. I have some candy bars as well." Hal produced several from his pocket and handed them over for storage with their gear.

The three men and Emma stripped and shifted to wolf, confirming Corey's suspicions. They weren't on suppression drugs, which was why they smelled wild and wolfish.

Questions trembled on the tip of his tongue. He forced them away. Now wasn't the time. But, fuck! What the hell sort of mess had he stepped into by returning to Yellowstone?

Chapter Twelve

"I THOUGHT EVERY WOLF took suppression drugs apart from those with official permission." Corey started his questions the second they boarded the bus.

R.J. ignored the demand for information and backed up the bus. When they turned onto the main road, Corey started to show his impatience.

"Aren't either of you going to answer me?"

"Every werewolf takes drugs unless they obtain official dispensation from the governing board. Every student who comes to Yellowstone has permission to go off the drugs for the duration of the course, but only if they sign an agreement stating they will recommence the drugs once they leave." Hal's matter-of-fact voice repeated the official stance on werewolves and suppression drugs.

"That's what my father told me. What are we having for dinner tonight?" Corey jiggled about on his seat then stretched his arms above his head. "I'm starving."

R.J. chuckled. "We're having whatever you decide to cook us for dinner. We forage for ourselves when we don't have students."

"I suppose I have to do the dishes too," Corey grumbled.

R.J.'s smile widened. God, he'd missed Corey, and while his return might have caused problems, he couldn't feel sorry. One thing was certain. He didn't intend to share a cabin with Emma tonight. At the first opportunity he'd grab Corey and find some privacy.

Back at camp, they went through Corey's belongings in silence. Each of them checked for anything out of the ordinary. They didn't find a thing.

"I think we're good," Hal said. "I'll call my contact anyway. See you later." He left the cabin and R.J. shut the door. He turned to face Corey, noting the new maturity in his face. The age difference didn't yawn so wide right now.

"What? Have I got a smudge on my face?" Corey swiped his hand over his cheek, a quizzical smile in place.

"I'm pleased you're here."

"Yeah?"

"Yeah." He reached over and turned the key, locking the door. The snip clicking into place sounded loud in the pulsing silence. "Take off your shirt."

Corey undressed at a leisurely pace, R.J. watching every button slip free of its hole, the gaping fabric giving him peek-a-boo glances of smooth flesh and muscular contours. "Tease."

Corey's throat moved in a swallow, making R.J. realize Corey wasn't as calm as he appeared. "I missed you." The shirt fell down his arms and slipped to the wooden floor.

R.J.'s gaze flitted down Corey's bare chest. Earlier when Corey had undressed, R.J. hadn't allowed his gaze to linger, not with the others present. But now they were alone, he indulged himself, taking his time to scan Corey's pectoral muscles and his trim stomach and abdomen. He moved close enough to touch, ran his hand over Corey's shoulder and trailed it down his chest, flicking flat nipples until Corey let out a low groan. Corey's scent flooded his lungs, a little different than he recalled, probably because of the suppression drugs.

"How come your father didn't get you to take the stronger drugs again?"

"No idea. Maybe he figured a half shift wouldn't happen again. This drug-taking stuff is crap. I don't understand why we can't learn to control our wolves and stop taking drugs."

"Too much money and power at stake. If humans

learned of our existence the president would be ousted."

Corey snorted. "So much for tolerance and accepting those who are different. What happened to judging on character rather than the color of our skin? I'm sure different species must fit into Martin Luther King's famous speech somehow."

"I don't want to talk politics."

"Me neither," Corey purred. "Did you notice I had lube?"

R.J. felt his lips curl into a grin. "No one ever accused me of being slow."

"What? No maidenly objections? What about Hal?"

"Hal knows everything."

"And?"

"And nothing," R.J. said. "I don't want to talk about Hal. I want action."

"Yeah?" Corey's dark brows rose in a faint challenge, practically daring him to do more.

"I want you, stripped naked and on the bottom bunk."

As R.J. said the words, Corey removed the rest of his clothes. The wooden bunk creaked when his weight settled in the middle of the mattress. He stared at R.J. with longing. Urgency thrummed in R.J. He ripped off his clothes and settled on the narrow mattress with Corey seconds later. He ran his hands over Corey's lean flanks, his muscular thighs, kissing everywhere he could reach. He nipped at soft flesh, laved the sting away with a swipe of his tongue. Corey clutched him close, his breathing harsh and urgent.

"I want you," Corey said. "I've dreamed of touching you again. God, I missed you."

Every hoarse word struck an echoing chord in R.J. This was *it* for him. Corey. He hugged him. "It hasn't been the same without you around. I missed running with you and sharing the small details of our days. I missed touching you. Your smiles." Their lips met, hurried and hungry. Hands grasped and squeezed. Corey's cock jabbed him in the stomach, leaving a wet smear across his skin.

He'd intended to lick and play, to tease and taunt Corey until he trembled with desperation. The kid had burrowed under his skin and clung like a burr attached to a sock.

This was a second chance, and one he didn't intend to forfeit without a fight.

He reached over and grabbed the lube, squirted a generous dollop into the palm of his hand. Beneath him Corey trembled in anticipation, with the same eagerness surging through his veins. He roughly parted Corey's legs and crawled between them.

"I can't wait to push into you." His rough voice trembled with need and desire. So much need. He couldn't remember ever needing sex this bad before. He didn't care how he got off as long as it happened with Corey.

"Do it." A begging note entered Corey's voice. "I've waited for this for days."

R.J. used a forefinger to stroke Corey's hole. Desperate for a deeper intimacy, he guided Corey's cock to his mouth and closed his eyes while he stroked, pushing lube into him, slicking Corey up for his possession. His tongue stroked the swollen crown, each lash in time with the intrusion of his finger.

Corey writhed under his attention, small groans and whimpers escaping him. Droplets of Corey's pre-come flowed across his tongue. Breathing hard, he ripped his mouth away. He fitted his cock to Corey's entrance and pushed inside until just his tip intruded, the tight muscles almost unbearable on his sensitive head.

"Don't stop," Corey wailed, wriggling and trying to draw him deeper. "Move. Do something. Please. I'm begging you."

"I want this to last." But unable to resist either Corey's pleas or his own needs, he drew back and thrust a little harder, battling the ring of muscle, savoring the heat. His hips jerked, pushing him deeper. Then he was inside Corey, balls deep and surrounded by clasping, throbbing heat. So good. His eyes closed and he blindly sought

Corey's mouth, kissing his shoulder, his neck and his jaw before managing to land one on his lips. Corey clutched him tightly, his manner possessive.

"Move. Please move," Corey pleaded against his lips, the garbled words scarcely recognizable.

"Corey. God." R.J. resisted the plea and continued to woo Corey with his lips, withdrawing and thrusting forward enough to keep them both on edge. When he noticed Corey reach for his cock, he knocked his hand away. "No, let me take care of you." He took him in his right hand, wrapping his fingers around Corey's warm flesh. He thrust harder, faster, getting closer and closer to losing control. His thrusts turned jerky, uneven. No finesse.

Corey's cock pulsed in his hand and he pumped his fingers up and down with firm strokes. Seconds later, Corey groaned and arched his back, forcing R.J. deep into his channel and the crown of his cock hard against the palm of his hand.

He rocked again and then Corey was coming. Liquid gushed into R.J.'s palm, the scent of their joining filling the air.

"You look beautiful when you come. I'll never tire of watching you." R.J. eased off on the hand action and put his energy into his thrusts. Hard and uncoordinated.

Good, so good he felt as if he were flying. Heat. It surrounded him, filled him. Pulled him under with its intensity.

Corey's channel clamped down, clutching him, massaging him and enticing him to fly higher. His balls tightened with his next thrust. He bit down on his lip, anxious to hold back his cry of pleasure. Then he realized he didn't have to hide any longer, not from Hal, not from himself. He pumped into Corey again and his climax rolled over him, semen shooting from him in hard spasms of pleasure. When they finally stopped, he slumped against Corey, exhausted yet invigorated at the same time.

Corey squeezed him, holding him close, and he felt as if he'd arrived home to a safe haven. R.J kissed his shoulder, his neck and finally Corey's lips. When R.J. lifted his head, he brushed his fingers across Corey's jaw, tenderness bringing a lump to his throat.

"Are you going to send me away?" Corey stilled his hand in the middle of R.J.'s sweaty back before resuming the comforting petting. "I...I want to stay."

"I know. I don't want you to go either, but what about your father?"

"I'm not a child anymore. I left home at eighteen and moved into my apartment. I haven't lived at home with my parents since then. He doesn't have anything to do with my decisions, even though he tries to boss me around."

"Does he know you're gay?"

"Nope," Corey said cheerfully. "I didn't think it was wise to share the information."

"We don't want your father around here," R.J. said, aiming for a diplomatic tone. Aw, hell. Maybe directness would work best. "It's kind of weird discussing your father when we're lying here naked."

"Is it because of the others? They're on the run or at least operating outside legal channels. They're not on suppression drugs."

R.J. pulled out of Corey, and instead of getting up, he tugged Corey back into his embrace. Funny, he'd never considered cuddling another man. With Corey the affection came naturally. "I'll tell you what I can before we grab a shower." He thumped his elbow against the wall and let out a yelp.

Corey chuckled and tried to shift over. "Maybe one day we can use a room with a big bed and a handy shower. A place where I can wander to the bathroom naked without having to dress first."

R.J. laughed but couldn't deny the rightness of the scene Corey described. "There's an underground movement in the States formed by a growing number of wolves who don't believe suppressing our natures is the right way to go."

"And they're...wow!" Corey clutched his shoulders. "Isn't that dangerous? What happens if you get caught?"

"Life's dangerous, Corey. You've lived in the city. You know what it's like."

"That's different."

"So you think it's okay for a few powerful werewolves to enforce their will on the others?"

"Of course not, but humans aren't ready to learn of our existence. Can you imagine the mass panic?"

"I don't object to laws, but we need fair ones that apply to everyone equally."

Teague stared through the bars of the cell, scarcely able to see through his swollen eyes. A guard strolled past the cell, his black Enforcer uniform a blur of color to him. Bastard. He'd taken great pleasure in cracking Teague's ribs, giving him the boot when he was down, writhing in pain from the Taser shot.

"You ready to talk yet?"

Teague turned carefully, biting his lip to hold back a cry of pain. A muffled groan escaped anyway, the throb in his bruised, swollen ribs sheer agony. Forcing his eyes open, he focused on Corey's father, uncertain of his course of action. One thing was certain. He couldn't take much more abuse.

An unearthly scream came from the far end of the corridor, shutting off abruptly. The acute silence was even worse than the screaming. It made Teague wonder, worry.

"Where is Corey?"

Grant Wilson stood at the doorway and studied him through the steel bars. His face bore not an ounce of pity. Teague recalled the brutal determination he'd seen the first day they'd taken him. Grant Wilson didn't like his son. Teague suspected he hated Corey. So why did he want him back so badly? Why did he try to exert his control over his son when it was obvious Corey wanted nothing to do with his father's world?

Teague didn't understand.

"I want to know the whereabouts of my son. Tell me and you can leave."

Intuition told Teague the man was lying. Even if he told him the truth, Grant Wilson didn't intend to release him. Teague knew too much, had heard too much in the days he'd spent down there.

The scientists were sadists. They enjoyed their work a little too much for his liking.

And the experiments they conducted down there in conjunction with the doctors—they couldn't be legal.

"I've told you. I don't know where Corey is. He didn't tell me where he was going and I didn't ask." The same line he'd maintained since they'd grabbed him at Corey's apartment.

"Here's the thing," Grant Wilson said. "I don't think you're telling the truth and, since I can't beat the answer out of you, I've come up with a new idea to make you talk."

Teague didn't answer. Nothing he said would make a difference so he saved his breath.

"I have your mother and siblings. They're staying with my wife and me. They're safe enough, for the moment." The threat dangled between them. The longer the silence, the more terror pulsed through Teague. His mother, his brothers. Fuck!

He owed Corey loyalty but this was his family.

"So I'll ask you again. Where is Corey?"

"I'm not telling you until my mother and brothers are in a safe place."

A sly grin crawled across Grant's face. "Safe is relative. They're safer where they are and my wife is happy having children to fuss over. My wife likes children."

Shit. Nothing he did would make this better. Maybe a partial answer. He closed his eyes, praying for guidance as he'd never prayed before.

"Stop fucking around. Where's Corey?"

Teague opened his eyes, shifting his weight for comfort. A shard of pain cut through his chest, bringing a groan.

"Corey went to New York."

Grant straightened, his eyes narrowing. "You said that earlier. Where in New York?"

"I don't know. I dropped him at the airport. That's all."

"What does he intend to do there?"

Teague shrugged, a moan breaking free as his ribs protested the move. "He said he wanted to find a job at one of the art galleries."

"Which one?"

"I don't know."

"Are you sure? I can arrange for your brothers to visit you here. They should probably have a check up with a doctor. Childhood diseases are rampant these days."

Hell. Fuck. Damn. What should he do?

"Where's Corey?" The quiet words stung like the lash of a whip across his flesh. He owed his loyalty to Corey but his brothers—he couldn't let them suffer. Not that he could trust Grant Wilson either. Between a ravine and a rabid wolf. No matter what he did, someone would get hurt.

Maybe he could stall for a little longer? Could he persuade Wilson to let his mother visit? No! That wouldn't work. Once she knew about this place, it would seal her fate. Wilson wouldn't let her leave.

"Corey is in New York. I don't know where he intended to stay. He wanted to get a job in another gallery." Teague risked a swift glance at Grant, his stomach sinking at the disbelief on the other man's hard visage. He looked away, galled he was unable to sustain the eye contact.

"Bullshit."

Teague flinched. "I don't know anything else."

"That's your final word."

"Yes." Teague hated bullies, and he understood why Corey wanted to move far away from this man. A streak of fear shot through him, producing a fine tremor, one the man didn't miss.

His mouth twisted, but it didn't approach anywhere near a smile. "I'll leave you to think."

Once Wilson's footsteps receded, Teague slumped against the nearest wall, a pained groan wrenching from deep in his throat. His stomach let out a protesting grumble. They'd given him water but no food. No suppression pills either, which worried him even more. If the world wasn't fuckin' screwed up with stupid laws, he might have attempted a shift to speed his healing. He didn't dwell on the thought. Shifting would only rain more trouble down on him. He sank down the wall, not even having the strength to make the three steps to the hard cot on the other side of his cell. Head hanging, his eyes closed. Someone cried in the cell next to him. Two men talked in low voices at the far end of the facility. Without warning, the screams started again. Full of anguish and suffering, they made the hairs at the back of his neck rise. A sense of hopelessness filled him and a tear flowed down his face.

The time passed. Teague fell into a shallow sleep, jerking awake with each fresh round of screaming.

Footsteps sounded—several men—but Teague couldn't summon the energy to lift his head, not even when they stopped outside his cell.

The door squeaked open and someone walked up to him. A kick hit him in the ribs. The second one struck him before he could escape.

"Get up." The harsh voice of the Enforcer who'd originally beat him sent a throb through his head. A third vicious kick didn't help.

Teague groaned, the pain in his ribs so bad he almost blacked out.

Rough arms grabbed him, holding him upright between them. Through narrowed eyes, he watched Wilson approach.

"This is your last chance to tell me Corey's location."

"I want to speak to my mother."

"Aw, he's a mommy's boy," one of the Enforcers said.

Grant produced a cell phone from his pocket. He opened it and spoke into the phone. "Home.

"Maya, can you put Helen on the line?"

Teague heard the other end of the conversation without difficulty. His mother really was staying with the Wilsons.

"Helen, I was wondering if you'd seen Teague. I wanted to talk to him about a job." The charm in his voice flowed down the line like sweet honey on a warm day.

"No, I haven't seen him. I'm worried. It's not like Teague to disappear."

Teague cried inside, wanting to warn her but powerless to halt her march toward danger.

"I'll put the word out in the pack," Grant said, his gaze on Teague. "Someone will have knowledge of his whereabouts. We parents do like to keep tabs on our children. I should have something for you later tonight."

"Thank you, Grant. I can't tell you how much I appreciate everything you've done for me and my children."

Teague wanted to shout out, to scream his mother was mistaken. She'd moved in with a monster, a man who didn't care about his own son. A man who was prepared to murder to obtain whatever he wanted.

"You don't have to thank me. It's my pleasure," Wilson said. "See you tonight." He disconnected the call and turned his full attention on Teague. "Last chance. Tell me where Corey is or you're dead. And after we kill you, your brothers and mother are next. Of course, I might toss your mother to the Enforcers for recreational purposes. She's beautiful, considering her age."

With a roar, Teague launched himself at Wilson. The Enforcers held him without difficulty and Wilson was never in any danger. Panting hard, Teague struggled, his fight weak. Ineffectual.

Wilson grabbed his shirt and yanked Teague closer until their faces almost touched. "Tell. Me. Where. Corey. Is."

"Yellowstone," Teague whispered, the fight draining out of him.

Wilson released him and he dropped to the ground. "Let's go."

"What about him?" one of the Enforcers asked.

"Leave him. We'll deal with him later."

Chapter Thirteen

Corey woke up curled around R.J. and remained motionless, so warm and cozy he hated to leave the narrow bunk.

"You awake?" R.J.'s warm breath tickled his ear.

"Yeah. I wish I was still asleep. I couldn't believe my ears when Emma volunteered to swap cabins."

"She makes out she's tough."

Corey stretched against R.J., flexing his muscles. "My presence is causing problems for you."

"I'm glad you came, kid."

A smile surfaced at the admission. "I know I can't stay permanently, but I thought about moving to Cody. They have a thriving art scene and you could visit when you have time off."

"You want to stay close to me?"

"You sound surprised." Corey wriggled around to face R.J. "I didn't go through this crap for a visit. I'm serious about you, R.J. If you don't feel the same way you'd better tell me now."

"Hell no. I want you here. Cody will work."

Corey grinned, the relief a real rush of blood to his brain. "Good."

"Good? That all you're gonna say?"

A laugh of pure pleasure escaped him this time. "I'd rather show you."

"We don't have time," R.J. said with regret. "I have stuff to prepare for the next intake of students, plus we have to get rid of our friends."

"Was Hal able to move up the schedule?"

"Yeah, but only one day. They're not leaving until tomorrow night."

"Guess I'll have to make do with a kiss." Corey squeezed closer, shamelessly rubbing their erections together.

R.J. cursed and Corey seized the moment, covering R.J.'s mouth with his. He snaked his hand between them to grasp both erections and started to pump slowly using their natural lube to ease the slide of his hand. To his surprise R.J. didn't struggle. He took control of the kiss, allowing Corey free rein with the hand job. Up and down.

A brief foray over the sensitive heads and back down again. He repeated the pattern until the pleasure filled every particle and cell of his body. Faster and faster his hand sped while their lips and tongues moved in lazy counterpoint. R.J. shattered first, release ripping through his big body. He tore their mouths apart and moaned, the muscles of his face and upper body tense with pleasure.

Corey exploded a few seconds later, going practically blind with the swell of satisfaction and contentment flooding him. His hand fell away from their cocks and he pressed closer to R.J., despite the messy come on their torsos. They kissed again, their mouths sliding together like old friends. Perfect.

A loud thump on their cabin door interrupted the lazy mood. "Hey, you love birds coming out any time soon?"

"Coming, Emma," Corey called.

"You'd better not," she snapped back. "That's way too much information for me this time of the morning. Hurry up. We have info." Emma's footsteps receded and still Corey didn't move.

"Come on, kid. We'd better move or she's likely to come back and burst inside."

"Scary."

"Yep, my sentiment exactly."

Corey moved first, rolling to his feet. He pulled on his

boxer-briefs, grabbed a towel and his toiletry bag. "You coming?"

"Yeah, though we'd better make the shower quick."

Fifteen minutes later they joined Hal, Emma and the three male werewolves for breakfast.

"What's the news?" Corey asked.

"Teague," Hal said.

Corey froze, almost dropping the milk he held in his right hand. He set the carton on the table without taking his gaze off Hal. "What about Teague?"

"We shouldn't tell him anything," one of the men said. "It's too dangerous. He's a Wilson and we shouldn't trust him."

"I understand where you're coming from," Corey said. "I get it. My father is a bastard and I'm an unknown quantity. I'll leave while you discuss details. Just tell me about Teague. Is he okay?"

"We have people inside your father's pack. One of them got Teague out of the cells before they killed him," Hal said.

R.J. seized Corey's hand and grasped it tight. The lump in Corey's throat swelled so much it was difficult to speak. "I..." He coughed and tried again. "My father put Teague in the holding cells?" Coldness seeped through him, starting at his toes and moving up his body until he shivered. "It's a hell-hole down there."

"How would you know?" one of the men demanded.

"I spent a few days in one of the cells. Fuck, I wouldn't wish that on anyone." Horror swelled inside him. "What did they do to him?"

"Tried to beat a confession out of him," Hal said.

"What—Aw, shit! Something to do with me?"

Hal met his gaze with calmness. "Your father wanted to discover your whereabouts."

"God, I can't believe my father. How bad is Teague? Is he gonna be okay?" Corey didn't understand any of this. His father had disowned him so why was he so desperate to find him again?

"Our medic thinks he'll recover," Hal said. "Your father is under the impression he's dead."

Corey didn't comprehend this either. He didn't ask questions, merely doctored his coffee with milk and wrapped his hands around the mug in an effort to get warm again.

"We need to find somewhere else to stay tonight until we can move on," one of the men said.

"Yes," Hal said, his voice heavy with regret. "I'm sorry."

"Not your fault," one of the men said.

Another of the men jerked his head in Corey's direction. "It's his fault."

Corey didn't argue because they were right. His father was out of control. His behavior toward Corey was one thing, but violence to his friend was unconscionable. "What about Teague's mother and brothers? Are they in danger?"

"I'll look into it." Emma shoved a notebook and pen toward him. "Write down everything you know about them and I'll do my best."

"Make it snappy," one of the men said. "We need to leave."

"I've already dropped—"

"Wait until the kid's gone," the snarly man warned.

Corey scrawled down everything he remembered and handed the notebook back to Emma. "Thanks." He picked up a plate of food and his coffee mug, ready to depart.

"Make sure you go a long way. We don't want you overhearing us."

Corey gave a clipped nod and kept walking until he stood on the far side of the camp. No longer hungry, he set his meal aside and stared across the grasslands and scrubby bushes, toward the mountains on the horizon. His father had really outdone himself this time.

Half an hour later, R.J. came out to join him.

"I might drive down to the other villages and check in

with the places I've left art. Can I borrow your SUV?"

"I need my vehicle but Hal has a car. You can probably borrow his. It's best if you make yourself scarce today. The less you learn of our activities the better."

"I'll go and see Hal now. I can go back inside, right?"

"Yeah." R.J. gave him a quick kiss and pulled a small bar of chocolate out of his pocket. He tucked it in Corey's waistband. "Take care, kid. I don't want anything to happen to you."

"Same goes," Corey said, his heart bursting with the need to tell R.J. exactly how he felt about him. Now wasn't the time. He'd tell him later once they were alone with no interruptions. He lifted a hand in farewell. "Thanks for the candy bar. See you later."

Thankfully, Hal handed over his car keys without a protest and Corey was soon driving away from Tower-Roosevelt toward Canyon Village. Mindful of the need to remain anonymous, he'd grabbed a cap and tucked his long hair up to change his normal appearance. His blue jeans and a souvenir T-shirt would help him blend in with the rest of the tourists, his camera the final element in his disguise. Checking with the lodges holding his paintings for sale wouldn't take long. The rest of his day he'd play tourist in truth, taking hundreds of photos, some of which he'd turn into paintings during the coming months.

Now that it was late in the season, some of the villages would soon close for the winter. There weren't as many people around, the roads noticeably quieter than when he was last there. Corey drove at a leisurely pace, stopping whenever a meadow or a stream caught his fancy. The wildflowers were mostly finished with a few straggling blooms giving a pinprick of color among the green meadows. At the Washburn Hot Springs overlook, Corey stopped again to gaze over Yellowstone caldera to the south. Today, despite the trials and tribulations, the sun shone brightly and the clear skies gave him a glimpse of the Teton Range in the distance. He took several photos before moving on.

The rest of the day passed in much the same manner. He dallied to watch a black bear and her two cubs wander through a clearing. He stood with other tourists while waiting for Old Faithful to blow, the water and steam shooting high into the air, the scent of sulfur making him sneeze. With the afternoon well under way, he drove around Yellowstone Lake. Along with photos of the lake and surrounding scenery, he captured shots of herons and an eagle perched in a tree.

Keen fishermen cast for fish and he even caught a glimpse of several kayaks before he turned his vehicle on the road back to Tower.

As he neared camp, his thoughts turned to the subject he'd attempted to avoid most of the day. His father. He didn't understand why his father would want him back so badly he'd have Teague tortured to learn of Corey's location. Why hadn't he grabbed him and locked him up to keep him in Los Angeles? Corey frowned as he pulled Hal's car into his parking space.

So many questions and he didn't have the slightest idea of the answers.

He'd never understood his father. Never. He flung his weight around, issuing edicts and never explained his reasoning. Yet no one questioned him. Even his second-in-command acceded to his father's every wish without an argument.

Maybe his departure had caused his father's status to diminish or something equally stupid.

Nah! Couldn't be.

The instant Corey climbed out of Hal's car his instincts prickled with warning. He froze, using every one of his senses to full effect. He inhaled, sifting through the scents to discover anything out of the ordinary. His wolf rippled beneath his skin, silently demanding he shift to face the lurking danger. No longer frightened by his dual nature, Corey commanded him with ease, silently reassuring his wolf until he settled with a grumpy snarl.

He scanned the vicinity. Nothing out of the ordinary. He sniffed again and smelled only the usual. After grabbing his camera and his day pack, he locked the car and pocketed the keys.

With the small hairs at the back of his neck still prickling, he glided silently forward. Someone had parked a gray rental car haphazardly in front of the main building. A man dressed in black stood by the car. He stood at ease, his back to Corey.

The low murmur of voices came from somewhere inside the building. Another man dressed in black stood by the open door. This one he recognized. An Enforcer—one of his father's personal security team.

His father had arrived in Yellowstone.

CHAPTER FOURTEEN

COREY'S FATHER WAS A real bastard.

R.J. had met a few during his brief time in the city. They didn't care about anyone or anything apart from power and the safety of their own skins. Like the majority of other wolves, Grant Wilson took suppression drugs.

His security guards—or at least the ones who entered the building with him—took the drugs too, although the scent of their wolves was stronger.

Hal sat behind his desk while R.J. stood against the office wall to his right. R.J. was glad Corey wasn't there. Hopefully they could get rid of Wilson and his goons before Corey arrived back for the day.

"Where is my son?"

"I've no idea," Hal said.

R.J. scowled at the man. One punch. That's all it would take. One blow to put a kink in Wilson's perfectly straight nose.

"Don't lie to me. I know my son is here and I want to see him."

Hal arched a brow. "Why?"

Wilson took a seat without invitation and crossed his legs before answering. "I'm worried about him."

"Corey's an adult. We enjoyed having him on the summer course, although I've no idea why you think he's here now."

"He intended to come here after he left New York."

Hal remained silent. R.J. waited, seeing little of Corey in his sire.

The door behind Wilson burst open. R.J. stiffened, ready to shout a warning.

Too late.

Corey brushed past the security guard and strode into Hal's office without hesitation. Part of R.J. filled with pride while the rest of him wanted to grab Corey and flee for safety. The impulse told him everything. He loved Corey and would do everything in his power to keep the younger man safe. Their relationship might have started as a fling but it had morphed into something else entirely.

He intended to keep Corey. A flash of humor filled him

then. He wasn't any better than Grant Wilson.

"You wanted to see me." Corey stalked toward his father without a hint of greeting on his face.

R.J. witnessed the flash of anger in Wilson's face. He'd prefer his son to cower at his feet like everyone else, expected it even.

"About time. Come, we'll return to Los Angeles today."

Corey stood tall and stared his father straight in the eye. "No. There's nothing for me in Los Angeles."

Wilson jerked his head at his security guard. The man walked up behind Corey and grabbed his arm. R.J. growled under his breath and straightened, ready to wade in and help.

"Wait." Hal's order stayed R.J.

Corey allowed the security guard to draw him closer before he struck, felling him with three quick punches before the guard could react. The man fell with a loud thump and didn't move again.

The office door flew open and another security guard stood in the doorway, weight balanced evenly on both feet while he summed up the situation.

"Out," Wilson said. "I wish to speak with my son in private."

R.J. tensed yet again as his gaze drifted over the new arrival. He knew this man.

Hal stood. "We'll wait in the dining room."

"I'd like R.J. to stay." Corey stalked to his side and turned to face his father.

"Alone, I said." Wilson obviously expected them to obey him but R.J. remained. If Corey wanted him to stay then that's what he'd do.

With a final warning glance at R.J., Hal left. The remaining security guard dragged his fallen comrade out, closing the door after him.

"You too."

Corey moved closer to R.J. "I have no secrets from R.J."

Something in his son's tone made Wilson's eyebrows rise. "You've changed. Grown a pair."

"Because I'm standing up to you?" Corey scoffed. "I don't suppose you're used to pack members doing that, especially with the Enforcers flanking you to provide muscle."

"Watch your mouth, boy."

To R.J.'s surprise, Corey sniffed but didn't make a reply.

"I require your presence in Los Angeles. You will start work with me and I will train you to take over the pack."

"You want Corey to take over the L.A. pack? From you?" R.J. registered the tightening of Wilson's mouth, the clenching of his hands at his sides. He didn't like R.J. butting in to a conversation he considered private.

Too bad.

"I don't want the position. I'm staying here." Corey's chin lifted and he spoke with calm confidence.

"Good God! You're just like him," Grant muttered and started pacing back and forth. "I thought—" He broke off and wheeled around to glare at them both.

Corey cocked his head and moved even closer to R.J. Each of R.J.'s inhalations smelled of Corey and a hint of chocolate. The scent both soothed and worried him.

"Who am I like?" Corey asked.

"Move away from him. You're behaving like a bloody queer."

Corey remained in place. "Maybe that's because I'm gay."

Shit. R.J. tensed, knowing what was coming even if Corey didn't seem to care.

"You're fuckin' joking," Grant snarled.

"Nope." Corey folded his arms across his chest and smiled. "You can go home now."

Wilson cursed. "Gay! The president of the United States has a gay son. Fuck, that's rich." He pounced and grabbed Corey, shaking him hard before he could wrench free.

Before R.J. intervened, Corey pushed back, flailing his arms and clipping his father on the chin. A growl escaped as he aimed a second punch. Wilson hit the wall, stunned by Corey's strength.

"You're not taking suppression pills." Wilson swiped at the trickle of blood coming from his nose.

"I'm taking the pills," Corey said.

"Bullshit. You shouldn't have strength like that. Keep away from me, dammit."

"I'm taking the damn pills," Corey snapped. "Tell me the truth for once. What the hell are you talking about? You're my father."

Wilson removed a pristine white handkerchief from his jacket pocket and glared at Corey. "Fuck no, and I'm glad. My son wouldn't turn out a fairy." He grimaced at the blood on his handkerchief and started when Corey snarled under his breath.

Stepson. Things started to make more sense. R.J. stole a swift glance at Corey.

"You're not my father. Color me relieved," Corey said, his tone mocking. "Why are you pretending if you hate my guts so much?"

R.J. got it before Corey. "For some reason your father—"

"He just said he's not my father," Corey snapped.

"He's using you somehow to get to the president," R.J. said. "Maybe blackmail."

The flicker of irritation in Grant Wilson confirmed he'd

hit on the truth.

"Is your wife Corey's mother?" R.J. asked.

"I don't have to answer your questions."

"Is she?" Corey asked.

"Yes."

Corey's eyes narrowed. "Did she have an affair?"

"She was pregnant when I married her."

"That must have pissed you off when you found out," Corey said.

Wilson shrugged. "Not particularly."

R.J. stared in disbelief. The man had schemed from the start, even before Corey's birth.

"Get out." The warning growl coming from deep in Corey's chest obviously worried Wilson because he backed up rapidly. R.J. had trouble withholding his grin. He was so proud of Corey. His wolf might lie close to the surface but Corey's control appeared absolute.

"I'm going," Wilson snarled. "Pansy."

"Call me whatever you want," Corey said. "At least I'm not a bully and a hypocrite."

"Don't bother coming back to L.A. or trying to contact your mother." The expression on Wilson's face was almost gloating. "I can't take responsibility for your safety there."

"I'm glad I never have to see your ugly face again, you sorry son of a bitch," Corey said, his tone hard and callous.

They watched Wilson back up to the door and wrench it open. His footsteps clattered across the wooden floor, signaling his departure. Seconds later a car started, although neither of them moved until they could no longer hear the motor.

Hal appeared in his office doorway. "Everything okay?"

"Not exactly," Corey muttered. "You can tell him everything. Hal should know the truth."

R.J. ran through everything they'd learned.

"Do you think he'll cause trouble?" Hal asked.

"I don't know him well enough to say," R.J. said.

"I embarrassed him," Corey said. "I think I'm okay as long as I stay away from his territory. I don't know what he had in mind. Maybe he can still go ahead with his plans."

"What are you going to do?" Hal asked.

Corey had no idea. None at all. How should he feel after learning the man he'd always called father wasn't related to him? "It's obvious my sperm donor didn't care enough to know me. I'll probably go ahead with my plans to find a place in Cody, maybe find a job in one of the galleries there."

"What about your mother? You could call her before your father gets home," Hal said.

Corey considered the suggestion. Part of him wanted answers, but why had his mother gone along with the pretense? If he was her son, why had she let Grant bully him all the time? Why hadn't she supported him like a mother should? Like Teague's mother. "I'll call her now."

"Do you want us to leave?" R.J. placed a hand on his shoulder in silent support. At least the news of his birth hadn't changed R.J.'s opinion of him.

"No. Stay and listen. If you think of any questions while I'm talking to her let me know." He picked up the phone and dialed his home. His mother picked up almost immediately. "Mom, it's me."

"Corey. Where are you?"

"New York," Corey said on instinct. "Mom, who is my real father?"

"What? Why on earth would you ask me that?"

"Stop lying. I know. Tell me the truth."

His mother started crying and Corey steeled his heart. "Is it true?"

"Yes." His mother's voice was scarcely louder than a whisper and Corey strained to hear her.

Something else occurred to Corey. "Does he know he has a son?"

"No."

Corey barely suppressed a snort. It was obvious Grant wanted to tell him or at least use Corey to exact some sort of pressure on presidential decisions. The idea sickened him. Grant had moved him around like a pawn on a chessboard, willing to sacrifice him whenever the mood suited him.

"Do you ever see him?"

"No. He was a friend of my brother's and used to come home with Charlie sometimes. We went out a few times, but I haven't seen him for years."

"So Grant knew about me from the start?"

"I couldn't marry a man without telling him the truth," his mother said, a trace of shock in her voice.

Corey's mouth twisted. She'd lied to her son without difficulty.

"Grant was in an accident. He can't have children of his own. He told me your arrival was a sign."

He wanted to howl. R.J. must have sensed his anguish because he moved closer and wrapped his arms around him, comforting him despite Hal's presence. "He was always strict with me."

"It didn't hurt you, Corey," his mother said. "He maintained discipline because he cared, because he wanted the best for you."

Yeah, right. "Did he know who my real father was from the start?"

"Of course. We don't have any secrets from each other."

So she knew about Teague. "Is Teague's mother still

staying with you?"

"No, it's the strangest thing. A man came to visit her. Her brother, she said, and she and the children left without an explanation. It was most peculiar and very rude!"

Corey knew Teague didn't have an uncle. He glanced at Hal and received a nod. The silent reassurance stilled the churning in the pit of his stomach. At least Teague's mother and brothers were safe. He didn't know how he'd manage to look Teague in the face if they met again. Teague's predicament was entirely his fault.

"Corey, I have to go. There's another call coming in. Look after yourself and call me again." The phone disconnected before Corey could respond. R.J. released him and Corey replaced the phone in the cradle, blinking to clear the film of moisture suddenly shrouding his vision.

"She didn't even ask where I was staying in New York or request a contact number."

"Try not to worry." Hal patted him on the shoulder. He glanced at R.J. "You have people who care for you. Blood ties aren't necessary to make a family."

R.J. winked at Hal. "I'm proof of that. My family is here with you and Hal."

R.J.'s words made him feel better, and when Hal nodded and squeezed his shoulder, the tears started to make his vision misty again.

"Everything will work out," Hal said gruffly. "I'll make sure they've left the park. We should be in business again, and our friends can come back to a bit of comfort before they move on."

Corey couldn't believe both R.J. and Hal would accept his past so easily. He watched Hal make a quick phone call and leave his office. "Is that it?"

"Corey, you're not your father. Stepfather," R.J. amended. "Hell, from what I've seen you don't take after your birth father either."

"I've never followed politics," Corey said.

"He's in favor of the suppression drugs," R.J. said.

"I hope Grant doesn't make trouble for Hal or put a stop to the courses here."

"He'll keep quiet because he knows we can reciprocate trouble-wise," R.J. said. "Come here, kid."

It was funny how an order from R.J. didn't make him want to dig in his heels. Corey didn't bother to fight. He stepped into R.J.'s embrace without a qualm. Lifting his head, he accepted the kiss, taking the implicit comfort. He sank against R.J.'s muscular chest and opened his mouth, lazily stroking his tongue against R.J.'s. A spike of sensation zapped his groin and blood started to fill his cock. He wriggled his hips against R.J., silently letting his lover know of his need.

R.J. laughed against his lips, pulling away slightly before pressing his forehead against Corey's. "Hold that thought, kid. Wait until after dinner."

"Promise?"

"Yeah."

Good enough for Corey. "Do you think I should keep taking my suppression pills?"

"If you stop you'd be breaking the law."

"Would anyone notice? Where is the nearest pack to here?"

"Jackson Hole. The drugs change a werewolf's scent. You smell a bit herby, which is probably from the hint of wolfbane they use in the pills."

"But in my pack... I mean, the wolves in the L.A. pack, all smell slightly different. I never noticed until I returned from Yellowstone."

"Which tells us there are different strengths of the suppression tablets available. When the drugs first came out we were promised equality."

"You can't be that old," Corey said in surprise.

A bark of laughter emerged from R.J. and his eyes crinkled at the corners. "Hell no. I learned it in history at school."

"Ah, that explains it. I was always doodling through

history and drew caricatures of my teacher and the other students. I spent a lot of time in detention."

"I need to cook dinner."

"I'll help," Corey said. "We can talk about what we're going to do to each other tonight once we're alone."

CHAPTER FIFTEEN

THEY CAME IN THE middle of the night.

Corey woke without warning, his heart pounding. A sound. Out of place. Foreign. He listened closely.

Every instinct screamed something was wrong. Corey pulled from R.J.'s embrace and slid from the narrow bed.

"What is it?" R.J. sounded tired, making Corey smirk.

His grin died when he glimpsed the gliding shadow not far from the cabin.

"R.J., someone's outside." As he spoke another figure separated from the shadow of a tree and drifted closer. "Do you have your phone? Ring Hal. We have company. Enforcers."

He heard R.J. speak to Hal. Seconds later he stood next to Corey at the small cabin window.

"Enforcers," Corey said again, a sick sensation in the pit of his stomach. This was his fault. He'd brought trouble to Yellowstone, because of his stepfather, because he was the president's son. He turned to grab some clothes.

"Don't bother dressing," R.J. said. "We'll shift to wolf. The bastards won't expect that."

R.J.'s phone gave a low buzz, indicating it was on vibrate. He snapped open his phone and spoke in a low tone before ending the call. "We're ready for them. They won't be expecting so many."

"So we're going to shift and spring out at them?"

"Yeah. They won't learn identities if we're in wolf form."

Grant wanted him dead or at least captured. Hell. He'd never be safe again. Corey's temper rose and his wolf writhed in irritation. Good. He hoped Grant was outside because he'd like to have another face-to-face meeting. Corey let his change flow smoothly through him. He growled low at the back of his throat. Beside him, R.J shifted and they both eased closer to the door. The minute an Enforcer opened the door they'd spring low, taking him by surprise.

Corey quivered in anticipation. He cocked his head, listening to the cautiously approaching footsteps. The handle twisted and the door inched open. The scent of sweat and gun oil hit him first, then the slightly herby scent he and R.J. had discussed earlier. The door eased open farther. R.J. nudged him gently and Corey tensed.

When the door didn't creak, the man opened it fully, his attention on the bunk beds in the room. The man took half a step forward and he and R.J. sprang together.

The man hit the ground. A startled cry burst from him, fading instantly when Corey grabbed him by the throat. Instinct took over. He bit down, tasted blood and yanked hard. A crack sounded. The man stilled.

R.J. growled at him and Corey let go, too psyched to experience horror. No time to worry. There were more.

They slipped through the darkness, both freezing when they glimpsed another man creeping stealthily in their direction.

Every lesson Hal and R.J. had taught him about hunting sprang to mind. He glanced at R.J. and they communicated silently with a mere glance. They parted, each approaching the man from a different direction.

Corey recognized this one. The man had struck him more than necessary when Corey became stuck in half-form.

Payback.

The man stumbled and Corey was on him. He slashed his claws across the man's back. A shot fired. Someone shouted. Corey snapped with his jaws, barely wincing when the man punched him in the ribs. No panic from this one. A soldier. Experienced. He thrashed around, attempting to throw Corey off.

A growl sounded.

Fierce.

Determined.

Behind him.

Finish him. Make it quick. Don't let your prey suffer.

Corey remembered the lectures. This man deserved to suffer. He'd probably helped torture Teague. The next growl was an order. Corey slashed with his claws, grabbed the man's throat and twisted. The taste of blood appalled him, thrilled him. Horrified him, but he didn't let release his grip.

This was war.

Slowly the fight faded from the man. Corey released his grasp, refusing to lap at the blood as his wolf wanted. Drinking blood would make *him* a beast.

R.J. appeared beside him. He snarled, a stern command to follow. Corey ran after R.J. toward the cabins housing the underground werewolves. They had everything under control.

So where was his stepfather?

Didn't like to do his own dirty work. That was clear.

Corey picked up the scent of one of the intruders

and followed the trail out of the camp. Behind him R.J. growled but Corey ignored him this time. This was about payback. Personal satisfaction.

He had a point to prove.

Corey picked up the pace, following the trail with ease. A car was parked down the road, the same car his stepfather had driven off in earlier in the day.

Before he could act, R.J. grabbed him. They rolled in a tangle of limbs. R.J. was bigger than him. Stronger, but Corey had fury on his side. He snarled and struggled against R.J.'s bulk.

"Who's there?"

Corey growled low and mean, fury and frustration lacing the snarl. He twisted, determined to get free of R.J.

A man appeared from the dark and Corey stilled. Immediately, R.J. grabbed his scruff and held him.

"Quick!" the Enforcer shouted. "They're after me."

Two big wolves sprang from the darkness, pouncing at the Enforcer before he could scream. Seconds later the man was still, the scent of fresh blood filling the air.

R.J. released Corey and charged his stepfather. Wilson ran around the car and fumbled with the driver's door. He finally managed to open it, cursing when R.J. snapped at his foot.

Corey rushed the car with the other wolves. The car

started but R.J. wrenched Wilson from the driver's seat, dragging him across the ground as if he weighed nothing more than a piece of paper.

Corey let out a sharp growl of disapproval. It was his right to put a stop to his stepfather's rule. He pounced at R.J. but one of the other wolves tackled him. Seconds later Grant Wilson was dead.

R.J stepped away from the body and morphed back to his human form. Furious, Corey shifted too.

"Why didn't you let me kill him? It was my right." His father—stepfather—had treated him like shit all his life, making him feel useless. Unloved. Not even his mother had stuck up for him because that bastard controlled their lives. Dammit, it had been his right to deal with his stepfather. He hadn't needed R.J. to protect him.

"You don't understand," R.J. said tersely. "Look, this isn't the time and place. Calm down."

Corey let out a derisive snort. What he really meant was he intended to do things his way. "I thought we'd already decided I wasn't a child. Don't treat me like one now."

"Then don't behave like one." R.J.'s glare stoked his temper.

Corey turned away, pissed. He couldn't talk to R.J. now, not with the agitation running through both him and his wolf. Before he could dart away, a hand curled around his left biceps.

"We'll walk back to the camp together."

Corey wrenched away, desperately reaching for control. He didn't want to fight with R.J. His stepfather was dead. This was a good thing. His mind accepted this truth, but deep in his heart he'd wanted to be the one to mete out justice. For him. For Teague. For the dozens of other poor werewolves Wilson had abused either indirectly or by setting his Enforcers on them. "Leave me alone." He took off at a sprint toward the camp. To his relief, this time R.J. let him go, probably assuming he'd return to their cabin. Instead Corey kept running and, once out of sight, shifted smoothly into wolf.

He needed to think. Get his head straight.

And somehow he needed to make R.J. understand he didn't need a keeper, someone to keep him safe. Corey wanted a lover, a man who stood at his side, shoulder to shoulder.

He was damn tired of people telling him what to do all the time.

R.J. TOOK A SHOWER, washing Wilson's blood off his body with calm, methodical strokes.

He'd killed the bastard.

Revenge.

Funny, he'd thought the knowledge would make him feel better. It didn't. The man who had killed his family was dead, and he felt nothing.

Instead he'd alienated Corey. Revenge hadn't brought his family back. They were still gone, dead, while he was very much alive.

R.J. dipped his head under the hot water, noting at the back of his mind the temperature had turned tepid. He must have been in the shower for longer than he'd thought. He turned off the tap and slicked his hands over his head. His hair needed a cut. His lips twisted in a spurt of amusement as he admitted the truth. Corey liked his hair longer, which was why he'd let it grow.

He'd do almost anything for Corey.

The amusement died as suddenly as it occurred. Corey would thank him later. Killing a man who'd had close ties to him, watching the life slip from his eyes, wasn't an experience the kid needed on his life resume.

"Yeah, right. Like that's the truth," he muttered as he grabbed his towel from the hook. When he'd seen the Enforcer's face, he'd realized Wilson was responsible for his family's death and simply acted without thought, without thinking of Corey's feelings on the subject.

If he'd stood in Corey's shoes he'd have wanted to take Wilson down himself.

Aw, fuck. He'd made a mess of this. No wonder Corey was pissed with him.

After toweling himself dry, he pulled on a pair of faded blue jeans and a T-shirt that had seen better days. A few minutes later, with his feet shod in boots, he grabbed his damp towel and toiletry bag and went to face Corey. Hopefully, he'd accept his apology once he explained things.

Corey wasn't in the cabin. He went looking, sticking his head in Hal's office.

"Hal, you seen Corey?"

"No."

He found Emma sitting in the lounge area near the dining room, flicking through a fashion magazine. She intercepted his smirk and snarled at him. "What you lookin' at?"

"Nothing. You seen Corey?"

"No, not since the fighting."

R.J. nodded. "Okay." That was over an hour ago. Where the hell was he? He searched the rest of the camp and when he couldn't find him, he paced the lounge area.

"Will you quit with the prowling?" Emma snapped at him.

"Corey hasn't come back."

"So?" one of the guys said. "He's an adult. He'll come back when he's ready."

R.J. stalked past Emma and dodged her kick, aimed at his ankles. "Did we get all the Enforcers?"

"According to the girl manning the park gate, there was a car with four people," Hal said.

Emma scoffed. "How come she remembers? Hundreds of people go through the gates every day."

"They were rude," Hal said. "Made it easy for her to remember them."

"Did she ask any nosy questions?" one of the men asked.

R.J. flung himself into a chair. They'd disposed of four bodies, which accounted for all of the werewolves. "Could there have been more?"

"More would be overkill," Emma said. "Think about it. They didn't know we were here. They thought it was you, Hal and Corey. Three Enforcers were ample protection for Wilson. He was taking a risk as it was because four men attracted attention. The girl at the gate remembered them. Stop worrying. Corey will be fine."

R.J. stared moodily at the door. They were right. Corey could look after himself.

SHELLEY MUNRO

AT NINE THE NEXT morning, Corey was still missing.

R.J. knocked on Hal's cabin door. "Corey isn't here," he said when Hal opened the door. "I'm going to try to track him before too many tourists pour into the park."

"I'll come and help."

"No, stay here. If I haven't found him by this afternoon, I'll come back for help. If I can't track him, I shouldn't be teaching tracking skills. He didn't come back and grab clothes."

"Which means he's in wolf form," Hal said.

"Yes."

"Okay, let me know if there's anything I can do to help."

"If I don't return by tonight, you'd better come looking for us."

"Make sure you're back tonight. I'm too old for all this excitement."

R.J. grinned despite his worry. Hal didn't seem much older than he'd appeared when R.J. first met him as a young eight-year-old kid, although he must be in his early fifties by now. "See you later."

R.J. strode from the camp to the spot where they'd met Wilson and his Enforcers the previous evening. There was no sign of Corey. After a swift glance in both directions, he ducked behind a tree and stripped. Seconds later, he called up his wolf and shifted. He embraced the discomfort of the change and the explosion of senses. One scent jumped out at him more than the others. Corey. With a wolfish smile of victory, he put his nose to the ground and followed the trail into the hills.

He trotted through the forest, the scent of pine heavy on the air. A fox darted across the track in front of him, scuttling into the undergrowth when he disturbed its foraging.

The trail continued through a clearing and past a small campground. An orange tent was pitched at the far end and the smoke of a camp fire curled into the air. Two adults sat by the fire and the scent of bacon distracted him for an instant. He should have stopped for breakfast.

Slinking low through the undergrowth, R.J. crept past the men, not picking up speed again until he was well clear. The incline of the terrain increased and he caught glimpses of the valley below. Still Corey's scent trail continued along the top of the ridge, past a recent landslide.

A sudden playful yip stopped him in his tracks. R.J. crept closer and looked down the trail. To his right there was a small clearing. He caught a flash of gray, and when he stalked closer he saw Corey. Every inch of tension left his body until he heard another yip. A small furry missile tore through the grass and sprang at Corey. Two more followed.

Wolf pups.

They couldn't be older than two or three months. R.J. froze, instinctively searching the vicinity for the pups' mother. How could Corey be so stupid? After the warnings he and Hal had given their students.

Where the hell was the mother?

R.J. scanned the grassy clearing and, once he sensed no danger, stalked closer, his belly low to the ground. And Corey wondered why everyone still treated him like a child.

Corey and the wolf pups scurried through the undergrowth then slowed, this time gliding silently. Perfect little hunters. As R.J. watched, it occurred to him Corey was patiently teaching the pups some of the hunting skills he and Hal had taught him. Perplexed, he settled on his belly, still watchful but more relaxed than a few minutes earlier.

The pups and Corey suddenly stopped their playing and turned to watch something coming toward them. Instead of fleeing, they moved toward the disturbance. The mother wolf trotted from behind a bush, a hare dangling from her mouth.

R.J. tensed, ready to intervene. The last thing he wanted to do was hurt any of the wolves but he would to keep Corey safe.

Along with the pups, Corey approached the mother

without fear. Totally thrown, R.J. watched the accident waiting to happen. The mother trotted over to Corey and dropped the rabbit at his feet. Astonishing R.J. even further, she rubbed her head against Corey in a gesture of welcome.

R.J. blinked. Hell. He'd listened to the stories Corey and Teague told after their unsuccessful hunt. Like the others, he'd dismissed them as tall tales. Now it was obvious they hadn't lied. He watched Corey take a token bite from the rabbit before he let out a whine inviting the pups to dine. Hell, he'd never have believed it if he hadn't seen Corey interact with his own eyes. He must have made a sound because the mother and Corey both tensed and turned in his direction. The pups scurried behind them and bobbed from his sight.

Slowly, R.J. stood and moved from hiding. He waited, unsure of what to do next. Corey made a soft almost inaudible bark and, after nuzzling him, the mother slinked into the undergrowth.

R.J. stepped closer and halted, waiting for Corey to approach him. Tentative and uncertain, for once in his life he wasn't sure what to do next. One thing he knew for sure—he wanted to spend time with Corey, living with him and loving him. But what did Corey want?

Before he could come to a decision, Corey approached

him. The wolf family's scent overlaid the one R.J. was familiar with. The pungent aroma wasn't unpleasant exactly, but it made R.J. more cautious. Corey kept walking toward him, silent yet intent. This wasn't the kid he'd first met. In his wolf form Corey showed confidence and, without warning, a spear of lust hit R.J. Hell, he wanted Corey. He was beautiful in both human and wolf forms.

Uncertainty hit R.J. when Corey stopped a few feet from him. He stared, trying to read Corey's mind. The kid had watched him kill his father the previous night. Stepfather, he amended, still trying to wrap his head around the tissue of lies the other man had spun. Yeah, if it were him he'd feel pissed. Uncertain and untrusting. He called, a soft cry somewhere between a whine and a growl. Corey's ears pricked. In answer he whined and leaped at R.J. like one of the boisterous pups.

Relief hit R.J. with the impact of the brick wall. If Corey met him halfway like this, they could work out the rest. Yeah, there were obstacles to their relationship, but surely compromise was possible.

The happy call of a bird and the chatter of a nearby squirrel told R.J. there was nothing amiss in the area. He dodged Corey's next dive and sprang in a return mock attack. They tussled playfully with a concert of mock growls and yips. R.J. used his greater weight and pushed Corey to the ground, grabbing him by the scruff to hold him down. Corey relaxed his body without warning, yielding.

Panting, R.J. relaxed too. Corey shivered beneath him, letting out a whine. Then he wriggled in a decidedly sexy way. R.J. froze in shock. Corey wriggled again, whining in a persistent demand.

He wanted sex? Now?

Thoughts whirred through R.J. so fast he could barely hear himself think. While his mind might fight the idea, his body had no scruples. His cock lengthened and his pulse rate jumped into a racy beat. A questioning growl escaped him. In answer Corey wriggled free. He twitched his tail and backed up to R.J. in silent demand.

Acting instinctively, R.J. covered him. His cock pierced Corey in a shallow thrust while excitement grabbed him by the chest. Pre-come eased his next thrust and Corey trembled beneath his body, silently encouraging him by not moving away. Wet heat surrounded his cock, the tight muscles of Corey's ass an added component to the lust sweeping R.J. The man in him countered the wildness of his wolf, counseling gentleness, and he managed this to a certain extent. Beneath him, the soft fur of Corey's back caressed his belly, the trembling excitement of his lover communicated with each renewed thrust. Man and beast combined, transporting him into a world of pleasure and loving, one he'd never experienced before. His balls tightened, lifted and seconds later he stilled atop Corey, exploding into an orgasm that seared the length of his body, made his muscles twitch and red explosions of light flare behind his closed eyes.

Gradually, he came back to himself and, aware of his weight, he pulled free. Immediately Corey backed away. Fear hit R.J. Had he hurt him?

The change rippled over Corey and his human form shimmered in front of R.J. Soon Corey stood in front of him, naked and fully aroused. He grinned, looking none the worse for his fucking in wolf form.

R.J. imagined his human form and shifted without taking his gaze off Corey. "Are you okay? Did I hurt you?" he asked hoarsely.

"It was amazing," Corey said. "Kiss me."

R.J. hesitated. "Are we all right about your father?"

"Stepfather." Corey didn't say anything more. He stepped closer to R.J. and kissed him—the determined kiss of a lover demanding sex.

R.J. wrapped his arms around Corey and surrendered to his demands. He kissed him back until the insistent press of Corey's cock distracted him. Pulling away, he led Corey to a grassy patch and pushed him down.

"What are you doing?" Corey smiled at him with lazy satisfaction.

"Why don't you wait and see?"

Corey's smile widened to a smirk. He placed his hands under his head and slowly stretched, flaunting his body without shame. R.J. settled at his side. Their mouths met, a slow mating of lips. R.J. took his time, teasing. Seducing. After a thorough kiss, he moved down Corey's body, nipping his chin, nibbling the tendons of his neck and laving the sting away with his tongue.

He licked Corey's flat nipples until they hardened. Although he'd explored Corey's body before and fucked him many times, this time felt different. More like a commitment. Frowning, he lifted his head.

"I love you, Corey. This isn't just about sex for me. It's not a fling."

"I wondered how long you'd take to realize you wanted me permanently."

A chuckle escaped R.J. No mistaking Corey's words for anything but smug. R.J. continued his exploring. A kiss here. A nip. A soothing lick. He continued in an erratic sequence so Corey never knew what to expect. The kid shuddered, his balls so tight they had to be painful. R.J. grinned, enjoying the sensual torture. He blew on one tight ball, licked the other before taking it into his mouth.

"R.J.," Corey said, his stomach tense while a drop of pre-come caught the sun and glinted. "Please, this is torture."

"I'm making memories," R.J. said, a jolt going through him at the truth he'd verbalized. It was true. He wanted to remember this day for a long time and he wanted Corey right there with him. "In fifty years time, I want us both to remember this day with a smile, remember how we felt and the pleasure."

Corey cracked open his eyes to stare at him. "Sounds like a marriage proposal."

"I'd marry you if I could," R.J. said. "I don't want anyone else but you."

Corey snorted, but he grinned a second later. "Took you long enough to realize."

"No one ever said I lacked the stubborn gene."

"Good," Corey said. "That's settled. Now about those memories?"

"Your father gave the order to have my family killed. I didn't realize he was responsible until I recognized one of the Enforcers protecting him. That's why I killed him."

"You needed closure."

"Yeah."

"I understand. It's enough to know he's dead and he

can't make any more werewolves suffer."

"Someone will replace him," R.J. said. "He must have a second-in-command. The L.A. pack is going to ask questions about his disappearance."

"True, but my father was always secretive. Hopefully that will work in our favor. I guess time will tell."

R.J. curled his fingers around the base of Corey's cock and squeezed. A noticeable jolt went through Corey. "I'm going to keep working with Hal in the underground movement. Suppressing our wolf natures isn't the right solution. It will be dangerous."

"I've been thinking about the future. I still intend to set up base in Cody. I can take the normal dose of suppression drug and keep shifting. None of the officials will be any the wiser, but I can help. I want to help. Oppression isn't the answer. Let's face it—we've all been brainwashed by a few wolves who want power."

"Your real father is one of them."

"He's not my father. The way I look at it, I'll be a special weapon in your arsenal. When the time is right we can use the knowledge to our advantage."

"I'm proud of you, Corey."

Corey beamed. "Enough to buy me some more chocolate? I've run out."

"I have a stash in my cabin with your name on it." So

euphoric he could burst, R.J. went back to seduction. He traced the prominent vein on the underside of Corey's cock before leaning down to take him in his mouth. Corey's flavor burst across his taste buds. Faintly salty with a hint of wild green. He licked the head and ridges before taking Corey's cock deep. He sucked and held Corey's hips firmly, controlling his thrusts, confining them to shallow ones when he knew Corey was getting desperate for release. He teased him to the point of torture then backed off to let him settle, repeating the process until Corey thrashed under him and pleaded for more.

With one hand, he caressed Corey's ass, probed him and pushed a finger inside. He pleasured Corey with mouth and finger in tandem, stroking his gland and teasing the delicate underside of his cock until Corey broke. A stream of semen hit the back of R.J.'s throat. Corey let out a hoarse shout and thrust deeper. R.J. held him, a sense of rightness filling him. When the spasms stopped, he separated their bodies and flopped down beside Corey.

"I'm glad you crashed into my life."

"Me too," Corey said. "I think I loved you from the moment I saw you. It was your bossy nature."

R.J. laughed, too satisfied to argue. He stared up at the blue sky and the surrounding trees, feeling one with nature. Something tickled his toes and he moved them only to feel the same sensation again.

Corey chuckled and R.J. lifted his head to see what was tickling him. One of the wolf pups had succumbed to curiosity. It lashed a pink tongue over R.J.'s toe while its mother watched from several feet away.

R.J. sat up slowly so he didn't frighten them. "You and Teague were telling the truth."

"Yep," Corey said. "When I needed to think I found myself here. The mother let me spend the night in her den."

"What about other humans?"

"Not many come up this way because there are no marked trails near here. She only trusted me and Teague because we freed her from the rock slide."

"I can keep an eye on her to make sure she doesn't get in trouble."

A human voice sounded in the distance and the wolf mother and her pups disappeared into the undergrowth. The surrounding birds and small creatures fell silent. R.J. and Corey both scrambled for cover, only coming out again when the two men disappeared around the corner.

"I guess that answers my concerns," R.J. said. "It must be our wolf side that makes them accept us."

"I don't know about you," Corey said, "but I'm starving. Race you back to camp." He shifted rapidly and sprinted away before R.J. could answer.

R.J. shook his head, contentment filling him as he embraced his wolf. Life with Corey would never be boring. After testing the air, he trotted from the clearing. Corey would challenge and love him. They'd probably argue and butt heads, but none of that scared R.J. The lone wolf in both of them had found a mate. Neither of them would be alone again.

THANK YOU FOR READING *Lone Wolf*. To keep up with new releases and book news please join my newsletter. (www.shelleymunro.com/newsletter/)

Also, I want to ask a favor. Word-of-mouth is crucial for an author to succeed. If you enjoyed *Lone Wolf*, please consider leaving a review. Even if it's only a few lines, it would be a tremendous help.

Please turn the page for a glimpse of *My Cat Nap*, a paranormal romance set in New Zealand plus an excerpt from *Fallen Idol*, a sci-fi romance.

Excerpt — My Cat Nap

Middlemarch Shifters, Book 12

NOTE: THIS BOOK CAN be read as a standalone.

"You smell good," the stranger said, his warm breath tickling across Rohan's ear.

A spear of pleasure shot through Rohan, sinking to his groin. A teenager's giggle brought him back and reminded him of the danger. Aware his sister had heard as well, Rohan started for the exit, shouldering most of the stranger's weight.

When they'd almost reached the car, Ambar ran ahead to unlock it. She opened the rear door and stood aside to let him help the stranger inside.

Rohan breathed deep, ultra aware of the attraction simmering between him and the stranger. With his arm around the man's shoulders, he could feel the heat coming off the shifter's body. Rohan's cock filled enough to worry him. He held his breath, trying to think of cold things, mindful of Ambar standing behind them. This wasn't the way he wanted her to find out about his preference for males. He scowled again. A tiger shifter and one he didn't know. What were the chances?

Grunting, he manhandled the stranger into the rear of Ambar's car, wishing they'd kept his SUV instead of selling it. That would have been much easier than squeezing the man into Ambar's small car. They'd sold Ambar's car as well, and the new owner would take possession on the day they left for Middlemarch. Rohan couldn't wait to take delivery of the new SUV they'd ordered in Dunedin.

"I like you," the stranger whispered. "Wanna fuck?"

Hell! Rohan went stock-still, his heart pounding so loud he was sure Ambar would hear the thumpity-thump as it beat against his ribs. And that wasn't all that was hard. His dick pressed against the fly of his jeans with an insistent pressure that made him want to rearrange himself for comfort. He cursed softly and attempted to move. The stranger gripped his shoulders and yanked him forward. Off balance, Rohan landed on top, both of them lying on the backseat. Seconds later the stranger kissed him on the mouth.

Rohan froze. Pull away. Laugh it off. Blame the kiss on the stranger not being in his right mind. All these thoughts flashed through Rohan's mind, yet he followed none of them. The warm touch of the male's lips moving beneath his held temptation, pushed against his restraint. His cock bucked, and when the stranger moved against him, Rohan gave up his losing fight. Rohan kissed him back despite the fact Ambar was watching. Despite the fact they were still parked in the hospital car park and in danger.

When Rohan finally lifted his head, they were both breathing hard. They stared at each other, the stranger lifting his hand to caress Rohan's cheek.

"Is there something you want to tell me?" Ambar asked in a choked voice. "Huh, maybe when we get home," she added in a hurry. "Get into the car properly. Now. And keep down. Grab the blanket and pull it over him. I'll drive."

Heart pumping with the urgency he heard in Ambar's voice, Rohan crawled inside, lifted the stranger's legs clear of the door, grabbed the tartan blanket from the back and spread it over them both. The car door slammed behind them.

"Kiss me again," the stranger said in a loud voice.

"We are really going to talk when we get home," Ambar said tartly.

The car started, turning sharply and throwing them both off balance.

"Drive slow and smoothly," Rohan said. "We don't want to attract attention."

"Shush. I need to concentrate."

Rohan shut up. A mistake because then he had time to appreciate his proximity to the stranger, take in his scent and feel the hardness of the man's erection pressing into his hip.

"Kiss—"

Rohan kissed him, telling himself it was a good way of shutting the stranger up. The first kiss had started off as a mashing of lips with no finesse. This one was different, as if the other man felt more alert. His tongue licked across the seam of Rohan's lips and he pressed the tip against the corner of Rohan's mouth. Immediately, Rohan envisaged penetration. A shot of pure lust converged in his gut, the reverberation ending in his balls. He gasped, feeling more turned-on than he could ever remember. And he didn't even know the man's name. The thought drifted away when pitched against the touch of the man's lips, sucking and nibbling on the tendons of his neck.

"I like kissing you," the stranger said. "You make me hot.

I can't wait to fuck you."

Rohan pulled away, breathing hard. He pressed his fingertips to the stranger's mouth, wanting him to quieten. Ambar didn't need to hear this stuff.

The stranger fell silent, and Rohan let his breath ease out in relief. Judging by the speed of the car, Ambar had left the parking area and was on the main road.

"Is anyone following?" he asked.

"I don't think so. I saw a couple of men run from the entrance. They were wearing uniforms, but I don't know if they were after us or not."

"Best to be sure," Rohan said.

"Yeah." A loud sigh sounded, and Rohan imagined Ambar had breathed hard enough to stir the lock of hair that sometimes fell over her forehead. "You'd better stay under the blanket and keep out of sight. If anyone is looking for us, a car with a driver and no passengers might throw them off."

A rough tongue dragged across his fingers, the abrasive sensation making him gasp. The stranger was going to kill him. Warm heat surrounded his fingers and the man sucked on them. Rohan cursed softly.

"Do I want to know why you're cursing?" Humor lurked in Ambar's voice this time, and although Rohan worried about the talk he knew was coming once they reached the safety of their home, he thought it might not be as bad as he'd imagined. She sounded curious and intrigued rather than disgusted.

They'd become close during childhood, teaming up against their parents' strict child-raising methods. Rohan had loved his parents, and he knew Ambar had as well, but there was no disputing they'd lived in the dark ages, believing in traditional roles for men and women and arranged marriages. Both still single by sheer luck and many arguments, they were ready for a new chapter in their lives. Rohan made a mental note to make sure he canceled the marriage broker. Ambar was still on the books. He'd ring India later today to ensure they were both free to follow their own paths.

The stranger swiped his tongue up and down Rohan's finger and sucked again.

"Quit that," Rohan snapped, snatching his fingers free of the stranger's mouth when all he really wanted to do was sink into the pleasure. He wanted to rip off the stranger's T-shirt and run his hands over his chest. Rohan blinked and stopped his thoughts above belt level. No point sinking into the gutter any farther than he'd already fallen.

"Almost back to the store," Ambar said. "For once I've struck most of the lights green."

"Is the sky falling?" Rohan asked. The rest of New Zealand made jokes about the constant snarl-up on Auckland roads, and for good reason. The traffic was horrendous.

"Oh shoot. There are two customers waiting in front of the store."

"Okay, give me a few minutes to get this guy up to the flat and you can open up. I'll get him settled and try to get some sense out of him. His name."

"You're gonna owe me," Ambar snapped. "One of the customers is Brian Gibson. I swear if he tries to touch my ass again I'm gonna deck him using every ounce of my strength. I won't care about holes in the walls or his head or anything else. Do you hear me?"

"Shrew, they can probably hear you on the other side of the world," the stranger said.

The car stopped so abruptly Rohan hit his head on the seat in front. The man grunted when his cock slammed into Rohan's hip.

"I hope that hurt," Ambar said sweetly. "Bro, you really owe me." The driver's door opened and closed.

Rohan pushed aside the blanket and shoved off the stranger. His face felt hot. Hell, his entire body shimmered with heat and a blind man would notice his erection. Ambar wasn't blind.

The rear door opened and Ambar peered at them both. Thankfully she didn't comment on their appearance. "Do you need help?"

"Just get the door for us. I'll help him up the stairs to the flat. As soon as I get him settled, I'll come down to help you in the store. You have my permission to hit Brian if he gets out of hand."

"Pretty," the stranger said.

Rohan hid the surge of disappointment behind a stoic face. That would be right. Half the men he met at the store had the hots for his sister. Why should this man be any different? Someone had drugged him and maybe worse. No wonder his head was addled. The kiss had meant nothing. Sighing, Rohan turned to find the man staring directly at him, not Ambar.

Ambar's eyes narrowed. She made a tiny noise at the back of her throat that could have meant anything and stomped over to the door leading directly to their flat above the store. Her expression told Rohan their talk would come before the day ended. He climbed out of the car and leaned back inside to grasp the other man.

"I can do it," the man said.

Rohan suppressed a smile at the snappy tone. It reminded him of a determined child, intent on testing his skills.

"Don't be long," Ambar called, disappearing inside.

Rohan watched the stranger closely, ready to grab him if he faltered. After long seconds, the man stood beside him. He wavered from side to side, looking like a sailor walking on land after a long sea voyage.

"How are you feeling?" Rohan asked. "What's your name? I'm Rohan Patel and that was my sister Ambar."

In the distance, he heard the roar of a lion, followed by the screech of primates. The familiar sounds coming from the nearby Auckland Zoo calmed the angst residing in his gut.

The stranger tensed, his head jerked and he turned to face the direction the sound came from. The lion roared again.

"Easy," Rohan said. "It's the lions at the zoo. The zoo isn't far from here." Not that Rohan blamed the man for his unease. Difficult not to feel a bit of anxiety, given the circumstances.

"Sister." A grin transformed the man's countenance as he turned his attention back on Rohan. "That's good to know. I thought you might have been married."

"No," Rohan said, holding back the surge of relief. "I wouldn't have kissed you if I was with anyone else." No sense getting ahead of himself. They knew nothing of this man, apart from his shifter status. They might go up in flames when they touched each other but that didn't mean they were compatible. "You didn't tell me your name."

"My name is..." The male trailed off, his brow furrowing in consternation. "My name is..." He wobbled and Rohan's arm shot out, slipping around his waist to steady him. "I don't know my name." A trace of panic coated his words, echoing in the stricken expression on his face.

"It's all right," Rohan soothed. Another layer to the puzzle. Maybe he'd hit his head and that had something to do with his memory problems. Although when they'd kissed, Rohan had noticed the faint sickly sweetness present when someone took drugs. Something else to check on... "Do you know where you come from? How you ended up in the hospital?"

The man's frown intensified. "I...I don't know. I can't remember anything."

Learn more about My Cat Nap
(www.shelleymunro.com/books/my-cat-nap/)

Excerpt — Fallen Idol

A Sci-Fi Romance

After climbing the dark stairwell, he exited on the fourth floor. There were six apartments on each floor. Rafi stalked down the wide passage toward number four, anticipation and apprehension skipping around inside him. Hell, seeing Roberto again was going to put him back at square one, ripping the scars from his wounded heart. But the idea of not seeing him—that was even worse.

He turned the corner and came to a halt. A pyramid of empty vroom flasks littered the passage outside number four. Rafi frowned and strode to the door. Vroom was a rough liquor produced on the planet Marchant. People became addicted to it if they weren't careful. Eyesight was affected. In extreme cases blindness occurred along with lack of coordination and muscle wastage. The muscle melted away, replaced by excess fat. Rafi checked the pile of bottles again and shook his head. Surely this pile didn't belong to Roberto. He knocked on the door.

"What the hell do you want?" a masculine voice demanded. "Go away."

Rafi pounded a little harder, a tiny grin playing across his lips. Roberto's voice. Familiar, it brought back memories. The husky growl still made his cock jump with anticipation. Rafi's grin died. *Friend's box, remember?* Roberto wasn't interested in him in that way and all the wishing in the world wouldn't change the facts.

"Go the fuck away!" Roberto's rough voice rumbled through the door, slightly slurred but definitely recognizable.

Rafi shuddered at the abrasive texture of his friend's sexy reply. He'd never met a male who turned him on so quickly with just a word. After taking a deep breath, Rafi knocked again.

The door flew open.

"I told you before, man. I have nothing left. You've taken everything."

Rafi gaped at his friend. He was still tall and dark, but the bronzed god from his memory had vanished. Roberto was pale as a ghost. An overweight ghost. His muscles had disappeared, sinking into inches of blubbery fat. The sight of Roberto's bare chest and protruding gut made Rafi faintly nauseous so he glanced at his friend's face instead. His dark hair was long, scruffy and lank as though it hadn't been washed for weeks. And his face—hell his beautiful face was bloated and puffy. One bloodshot blue eye scowled at him while the other was black and almost swollen shut. Roberto's jaw was swollen too, and when Rafi studied his body again, he noticed bruises. Someone had bashed his friend and done a pretty good job of it.

"Roberto," Rafi said. He stood in the open doorway, uncertain for once in his life. He still didn't know where to look. Didn't Roberto have some clothes? That belly...it... Hell! It needed camouflage. Really badly. Rafi stared with fascinated horror as Roberto's belly jiggled when he inhaled.

His crew would have gaped with open mouths if they'd seen their captain appearing so indecisive. In the past, the two men would have exchanged a quick hug and clapped each other over the back. Rafi would have savored the moment as he usually did. He'd imagined the feel of Roberto's arms around him from the moment he'd decided to look his friend up between trips to the outer territories. Instead, there was awkwardness. Rafi didn't know what the hell to do. It was difficult looking at that blubber, but touching it? He shuddered inwardly and continued to hover outside the apartment. Part of him wanted to leave, to run away, but no, he couldn't do that. He refused to run away. His legs remained firmly planted outside the apartment while his mind told him to deal with it. No matter what, or how he looked, Roberto was still his friend.

"Rafi?"

Rafi tensed and steeled himself, forcing his real feelings deep so nothing showed from the outside. "Yeah, man. I stopped by the Gratham Apartments. One of the security men said you'd moved here." Not bad. His voice had sounded calm. Even.

"I don't suppose you'd leave if I asked you?" A tinge of shame colored Roberto's cheeks and his gaze slid away to stare at the floor.

Rafi forced himself to look his friend in the face. He was so...so... Hell, he reminded Rafi of a bloated whale. His gaze flitted across Roberto's face before darting over his friend's shoulder to study what he could of the apartment. Another heap of opaque vroom flasks lay beside a wooden chair. The apartment was filthy and offended Rafi's nose. Soy dog wrappers littered the cheap plastic table. An open suitcase lay on the floor and the contents were strewn across the grubby gray floor in haphazard heaps. Rafi gave a cautious sniff before frowning. The smell could be coming from Roberto. He wasn't certain, but whatever the source, it was disgusting.

Rafi straightened and forced himself to look Roberto in the face again. "Why would I leave? Roberto, I came to see you." Roberto was his friend, and he was a friend in need.

Roberto didn't look convinced. "My name's Bob," he said. "I was born Bob and looks like I'll die Bob." Bitterness shaded his voice. "Call me Bob, like you used to when we were kids."

"Ah, sure." Rafi frowned. What the hell was going on? What had happened to his friend since his well-publicized injury? Roberto had always acted with confidence and known what he wanted from life. Ambitious from childhood, he'd set his mind on becoming a successful sex competitor and focused on his goal one hundred percent until he'd succeeded. He hadn't minded when Bob had wanted everyone to call him by his stage name. Rafi knew about being consumed by a dream, wanting to live it and become immersed in the success, which is why he'd understood Roberto. Rafi had always wanted to explore the uncharted territories. Maybe one day.

Since it didn't look as though Bob was going to let him inside, Rafi took matters into his own hands. He stalked past Roberto...Bob and recoiled at the stench. Gasping, he headed straight for the window.

"Won't open. It's nailed shut," Bob said seconds before Rafi attempted to open it.

Rafi turned to glance at his friend again. "Man, you need to do a little cleaning." His eyes streamed and he breathed shallowly through his mouth, trying to filter out the worst of the smell. Didn't work. "And you need a bath."

"Keeps the debt collectors away." Bob's top lip curled upward, and he shrugged with unconcern. "Most of them." His blasé attitude was spoiled when he winced. Obviously the bruises on his body were still painful.

"Get cleaned up and I'll buy you a meal." Rafi was starting to feel pissed with his friend. He'd been looking forward to seeing Roberto, and even though he'd known Roberto wasn't interested in him in the same way, he'd expected to slip right into their easy friendship. Rafi's gaze slid across Roberto's pale, bloated face. This man was a stranger.

"Go out?" Bob made a theatrical gesture with his hands and struck a pose, one Rafi had seen him make onstage. He remembered the surge of jealousy he'd felt when Roberto's female partner had trailed her hands over Roberto...ah...Bob's tanned, muscular body when he'd stood in exactly the same way. Yeah, they'd looked great together on the stage but it hadn't lessened Rafi's longing.

He'd imagined thrusting into Bob, running his hands over the smooth muscles, clutching the weight of his cock in his hands...

"I don't have a thing to wear," his friend said in a harsh voice.

Learn more about Fallen Idol
www.shelleymunro.com/books/fallen-idol/

About Author

USA Today bestselling author Shelley Munro lives in Auckland, the City of Sails, with her husband and a cheeky Jack Russell/mystery breed dog.

Typical New Zealanders, Shelley and her husband left home for their big OE soon after they married (translation of New Zealand speak - big overseas experience). A twelve-month-long adventure lengthened to six years of roaming the world. Enduring memories include being almost sat on by a mountain gorilla in Rwanda, lazing on white sandy beaches in India, whale watching in Alaska, searching for leprechauns in Ireland, and dealing with ghosts in an English pub.

While travel is still a big attraction, these days Shelley is most likely found in front of her computer following another love - that of writing stories of contemporary and paranormal romance and adventure. Other interests include watching rugby (strictly for research purposes), cycling, playing croquet and the ukelele, and curling up with an enjoyable book.

Visit Shelley at her Website

www.shelleymunro.com

Join Shelley's Newsletter

www.shelleymunro.com/newsletter

Follow Shelley at Bookbub

www.bookbub.com/authors/shelley-munro

ALSO BY SHELLEY

Sports Romances
No Defense
Best Man
Eye on the Ball

Paranormal Romances
Curse Across Time
Lone Wolf
Seeking Kokopelli
Last Wish
Fallen Idol

Paranormal Box Set
Under His Spell

www.ingramcontent.com/pod-product-compliance
Lightning Source LLC
Chambersburg PA
CBHW020944260626
47169CB00006B/1809